About the Author

An intelligent young man, with a talent for numbers, who is on the journey to become a charted accountant. He has a keen interest in human psychology, and in the co-relation between the beauty of romance and the darkness of destruction. Born with the talent for the art of storytelling and improvisation, Archie is looking to further his talents in the art form, with this, what he hopes will be, the first of many works of fiction.

Love... The Greatest Crime

Archie Paterson

Love... The Greatest Crime

Olympia Publishers
London

www.olympiapublishers.com
OLYMPIA PAPERBACK EDITION

Copyright © Archie Paterson 2024

The right of Archie Paterson to be identified as author of
this work has been asserted in accordance with sections 77 and 78 of
the Copyright, Designs and Patents Act 1988.

All Rights Reserved

No reproduction, copy or transmission of this publication
may be made without written permission.
No paragraph of this publication may be reproduced,
copied or transmitted save with the written permission of the publisher,
or in accordance with the provisions
of the Copyright Act 1956 (as amended).

Any person who commits any unauthorised act in relation to
this publication may be liable to criminal
prosecution and civil claims for damage.

A CIP catalogue record for this title is
available from the British Library.

ISBN: 978-1-80439-788-6

This is a work of fiction.
Names, characters, places and incidents originate from the writer's
imagination. Any resemblance to actual persons, living or dead, is
purely coincidental.

First Published in 2024

Olympia Publishers
Tallis House
2 Tallis Street
London
EC4Y 0AB

Printed in Great Britain

Dedication

For my mother, SP. Thank you for always supporting me.

Chapter 1

Love... the most complex human emotion. One of the greatest clichés of our existence. It promises us great beauty and happiness but in the greater scheme of things, brings pain and suffering.

The human body has two major control organs, the brain and the heart. They are at war for control of the body. The brain wants you to be logical and do what would be best for the most in a situation, while the heart wants you to be happy and leads one to make decisions that are irrational and illogical. What a clever-stupid species we are, it's no wonder that we are the only creatures on this planet that play no 'building' role in our eco-system.

Now let me tell you a tale. A tale of a classic guy who can agree with what many of us claim. That love is a deceptive emotion and causes more problems than happiness. It can actually bring one to their demise.

Like most classic love stories, this tale starts at high school. Our hero, Richard 'Castle' King, a descendant of the royal family of England, hence the nickname "Castle", went to an average private South African high school called Cape high, in Cape Town. Now if you are wondering why a person tied to English royalty would go to an average high school in South Africa, it's because he was so far off the line in the family that he really had no real claim to any of the royal possessions.

He was nothing short of a genius. His family and educators

all knew that he would make a success of his life, and so did he. Until one huge obstacle stood before him when he met a very special young lady named Sylvia 'Becky' Beckette. His perfect equal and opposite. You see while they were both geniuses, but they each had one very big weakness. Richard's was his language. He was brilliant at English as you could probably assume but struggled with Afrikaans, which he had to do no matter which school he went to. Sylvia on the other hand was also a genius but struggled with Mathematics. Bizarrely though Sylvia was a master in the art of Afrikaans, and Richard a Master of Mathematics. As you can probably guess this made their meeting inevitable. Upon meeting her for the first time, Richard... lost it. He felt weird. Like for the few seconds he got to lay his eyes on her all was in perfect balance in the world.

He didn't know what to call it. He had never felt that way before.

That very day, when he got home, he spoke to his older sister and she said to him, "That is called 'Love'."

Love? Richard thought to himself. He had heard of this once before in a fairy tale his sister used to read to him each night before he went to bed, but he never believed in any of it. To him, it was always nothing but a big fairy tale, but now he asked himself... could it be real?

His brain and heart began to feud over the matter and, foolishly, he decided to side with his heart.

The very next day, he searched for her at school. He eventually found her, drinking water and staring at her smartphone. He didn't hesitate to go over to her and introduce himself to her. He succeeded at making a good first impression and about a week later, they were actually very good friends.

Richard seemed very good at playing the game of love this

far... but was he really? He found himself doing his accounting homework at his desk one night and realised something... something important. He realised that he was... a... coward. He had had plenty of opportunities in the week that had passed to tell Sylvia how he felt about her, but he didn't have the courage to do it.

As he worked through his ledger, he tried to convince himself to tell her the next day. He knew he wasn't the only guy at school who fancied her, and he needed to make his move before anyone else did.

Days went by, each day he grew closer to her but he never managed to sum up the balls to do it.

They had a conversation one afternoon, after school, about their futures. Richard told her that he was planning to enter the law or accounting field. He had a passion for both money and he enjoyed the drama and adrenaline of the court rooms. Sylvia told him that she planned to enter the civil engineering field, which involves people who build houses and things like that.

Richard looked on at her, now deep in emotional shock. He realised that there was now an obstacle in his way. If they planned to lead two different lives, it meant that they would most likely go to two separate universities the following year. With the year being more or less half over already, it meant he would have to profess his feelings for her soon.

The perfect opportunity came to his mind. *The Matric Dance!* he thought to himself. They would soon have their matric dance, which meant he would have the perfect opportunity to 'get romantic' with her. It was the best, and really the only ace he had up his sleeve. But waiting that month before the dance cost him much more than he had bargained for. Dylan, a long-term rival of Richards, who was also infatuated with Sylvia, had been brave and asked her out on a date. For Dylan, it went pretty well. They really clicked on that one date and arranged to be partners for the matric dance. Sylvia and Richard, being close, told each other pretty much everything that happened in their lives and as such, so Sylvia told him about the date and how she was now dating Dylan. The shock on Richard's face and the scare in his heart in that moment were beyond compare. Especially since Richard planned to ask her to the dance that afternoon. Instant heartbreak, and Sylvia had no clue of the pain that went through her friend that day.

Later that day, emotionally wounded Richard sat by the pool of his house and considered what to do next. He decided that despite the fact that she was with Dylan, he was going to tell her how he felt about her and ask her to the matric dance with him, the very next day.

Disaster was upon him…

The next day, he asked her to meet him on the rugby field, where they weren't allowed, so that they could have some privacy. She agreed. On the rugby field that day, he poured his heart out to her and put his arms around her waist and said, "I love you." A second later, he found himself staring down at the grass beneath him, as Sylvia had just slapped him in the face right across his cheek.

As he turned his face to look back at her, she said to him, "You and I… it's NEVER going to happen." Then she turned around and left.

The pink impression of a hand left on his face from the slap was nothing compared to the bullet that had passed through his heart. The ultimate pain that a man can feel had just fallen upon him. Not a kick in the balls. Rejection.

Rejection can turn the nicest man into a complete monster.

It shatters his confidence and bursts his ego. With that... his world was destroyed.

Now all he wanted was to get his matric certificate and move on with his life.

His wish didn't take long to come true. Soon, he had written his matric exams and earned his certificate. With that, he was free.

Sylvia too passed her matric and moved on to university, to jump-start her life. She went to study civil engineering and Richard well... his Afrikaans mark was a bit too low for him to study law so he followed his second passion. The passion for money and with that studied accounting.

Four years later, he was a full-fledged charted accountant. One of the best if not THE best. There wasn't one financial institution in the country that wasn't willing to hire him. He was a multi-millionaire within two years of starting to practice as an accountant. However, there was still something he felt lacking...

Richard, while not being able to study law, still possessed a deep passion for it and found a way to fulfil it. He was still brilliant at English as a language and he used that talent to write books.

Surprisingly, he really enjoyed writing, even though he hated reading. He followed cases that he attended in the local court and used them as inspiration for his books.

He quickly became a very famous author and novelist. He released five books in the following two years and all of which were best sellers. The royalties from his books were almost as much as his income from his accounting practice.

It was now eight years since he had last seen Sylvia. He lived in an ultra-luxurious penthouse on the top floor of a skyscraper in New York City. He had left South Africa behind him after his studies. He lived with his seven-year-old daughter, who he shared with an ex-girlfriend from his first year at university, and his mother. His baby momma had run off before he left South Africa which left him with his daughter.

His mother was proud of her son who was a success and very responsible with his daughter, but just like all single mothers with sons, she was eager for him to get married. Richard on the other hand had no interest in marriage or relationships, he enjoyed his life just as it was.

But like all good things, it came to an end one fateful day...

As he sat in his office one afternoon, dealing with client after client until his PA, Monica, buzzed him on the intercom and said, "Sir, there is a detective here who wants to see you."

Puzzled and confused by why a detective might want to see him, he buzzed the intercom button and said, "Let him up."

He rotated his chair to stare out of the window, and to face away from his office door to think about why a detective would want to see him. He knew for a fact that he had not broken the law.

He heard footsteps at his door and then heard someone say "Mr King?" in a sweet and soothing voice. He realised it was a woman, which caught him off guard. He rotated round to greet her and as he did... instant shock...

"Sylvia?" he said in shock and surprise.

"It's 'Detective Beckette' nowadays," she responded bluntly.

In his surprise to see her in his office, he stood still and eventually, she asked if she may have a seat since he had not yet offered her to sit. He agreed and said that it was good to see her again after the past eight years.

"Let's just keep things professional, shall we? I'm here on

official police business."

Richard looked at her and bluntly asked, "What can I do for you?"

Sylvia explained to him that she was currently working on a homicide case and she needed an expert to analyse a major financial transaction that could be related. She also made it clear to him that she had not come to see him because they were old friends and figured, therefore, he would agree, it was because he was the best in all of NY.

He agreed and she gave him a hard drive to inspect. He told her that he would be done with it in three days. Sylvia then stood up to leave and he interrupted her. He asked, "Hey, wait, Sylvia. What exactly is going on?" in a confused tone.

Her response was that she wasn't allowed to discuss police matters with him, trying to divert his question, even though she knew what he meant. He was referring to why she was a homicide detective in New York, instead of a civil engineer in South Africa.

When he specified to what he was referring, she sat down on the velvet red sofa in his office and exhaled heavily. She then told him a sad and heartening story of how her father won a custody battle against her mother over her and then she and her dad moved to New York so she could get a better-quality education than in South Africa. Then, soon after the move, she went out one night to go drinking with her friends, she left her dad at home where he was murdered, for no clear reason. A year then passed with no new evidence and the police filed the case among the cold cases. She then decided to quit her civil engineering course and go to the police academy, with the goal of making sure that others did not have to go through the same thing.

Touched by the story, Richard offered to take her out for a

drink, but Sylvia refused and left his office and gave a final remark, "Just tell me when you are done with your analysis!"

Once she left, he went to his chair, packed his laptop bag, took the hard drive and left to go home.

As he went through the hard drive at home that evening, drinking his whiskey, he was extremely distracted by the memories of professing his love to her eight years ago replaying themselves in his head. '...*you and I... it's NEVER going to happen'* **SLAP!** *'You and I... NEVER happen!'* *'NEVER happen!'* *'NEVER happen!'* **SLAP!**

He was brought away from the replaying memory by the sound of this mother asking for his opinion on her new dress. Eventually, he decided to go to sleep and look through the drive the next day.

Falling asleep was impossible that night as the memory continued to replay itself. Eventually, he gave in and listened to what his heart was trying to whisper to him. He understood that his heart wanted him to try to get with Sylvia again as he still had feelings for her buried deep in his heart. His brain on the other hand tried to convince him not to by reminding him of the pain this same woman had brought him almost a decade ago. Eventually, he succumbed to his heart and chose to obey it.

He had become such a success in his life that he began to feel a bit bored with it. He already had enough money to buy all of the United States if he wanted to. Maybe it was time to try and complete his life by having a woman that he could love. He had decided that he would try to become her man again. Of course, with a mother who was so eager for him to marry, it would also mean that if he succeeded, he would finally have peace in his own house when she moved out. But as for now, she couldn't know that her son was... in love.

Firstly, though he would need a plan. Once he gave her the result of his analysis on the drive, they would no longer have a connection. Which made both time and opportunity scarce. What to do... they lived in two different worlds, career-wise. One was a cop, the other an accountant and writer. What a mouthful...

The next morning, he went to his computer and started going through the hard drive again with his head still weighted down by his thoughts. He sat for hours on end and eventually slapped his own forehead, in frustration. He was on the verge of giving up, until...

He noticed a weird transaction. A very large sum of money that didn't seem to have an origin. He followed the money and discovered that it was washed through a number of fronts, to try and hide where it came from. Finally, he was getting somewhere, where exactly... he didn't know but was excited to find out.

Finally, after hours of tracing, he found the money had originated from an offshore account, which meant it was laundered. Eventually, he got the name of the account holder... "Michael Larry."

Michael Larry? he thought to himself. *I've heard that name before.* He wandered the house and took a sip of his Corona, pondering at the thought of where he had heard the name Michael Larry before.

He eventually gave up the thought and decided to go to bed. Before that, he called Sylvia, to say he had found something, and wanted to tell her over a coffee the following morning.

He was just an accountant, after all, and finding the name was good enough to give Sylvia. She told him that she was going to the courthouse the following morning for a parole hearing so she could only meet him in the afternoon. They hung up and as Richard stood over his bed, he thought to himself, *"Court... court... court."*

Of course! Michael Larry! He had heard that name in one of the trials he had attended while looking for inspiration for his previous book!

Thinking more deeply, he realised something. Maybe he had an opportunity that he *could* exploit already. It was all right in front of him.

Tomorrow afternoon was going to be a moment where he would make his grand mark. He had a plan...

Chapter 2

The next morning, he woke up, got dressed, ate breakfast and left the penthouse, full of confidence. He had a plan to kill three birds with one stone.

He waited at the coffee shop, with a croissant and a latte, for Sylvia to arrive.

As Sylvia pulled up outside, she exhaled heavily and said to herself in her head, "*Let's get what we need from him and be done with it all. Then I'll never have to speak to him again.*"

She went in and found him sitting by the window. In an attempt to be friendly with her, Richard asked how the parole hearing went.

She responded with the remark, "Just tell me what you found, Richard."

He nodded, exhaled and said, "Thirty-eight thousand dollars, laundered, originating from one Michael Larry." He slid the hard drive across the table to hand it back to her.

Then, she stood and said, "Thank you, Mr King."

As she turned to walk away from him, he held her arm and said, "Wait! There's more."

She sat down and pointed out her watch to him, so as to say "Come on then, tell me."

"Michael Larry is a convicted criminal. He was found guilty of running an agency that ran contract killers. He appeared in front of the grand jury six months ago. He is currently serving life in prison in San Quentin state prison," Richard told her.

Upon hearing this, Sylvia looked at him with a surprised expression and asked him how he knew this. Richard then told her that he had attended his trial while looking for inspiration for his most recent book that he had launched.

"Wait. So, you are saying that the man I am currently investigating could very well be the killer, who was hired to kill my victim and was working for Michael's agency?"

Richard nodded his head with a slight grin on his face. Sylvia then thanked him for his help and began to walk to the door. Richard ran after her and called out to her as she put one leg into her car. When she stopped to hear what he had to say, Richard froze and simply said, "It was nice seeing you again."

Sylvia then replied, "Likewise." She did enjoy seeing her old friend again, after so long, but she was afraid that history would repeat itself and he would fall in love with her all over again. That's why she wanted to be done with him as soon as possible.

Richard got into his Benz and gently hit his forehead against the steering wheel, in defeat. He had just thrown his perfect plan out the window by freezing up when talking to her. He had something to ask of her and he would now have to find a different way to do it.

When he got home in the evening, he hung his suit jacket on the coat hanger and went to the fridge to get a Corona. As he sipped away at it, there was a knock at his door. Slightly drunk, he yelled out, "Forgot your keys again, Mother?" thinking it was his mother and daughter arriving home. How wrong he was…

It was Sylvia, with three policemen in bulletproof vests. "Oh, Sylvia. Uhmm, what… what… what can I do for you?"

She didn't even answer his question. She just said, "Mr King. You are under arrest for lying to an officer of the law, and for attempting to defeat the ends of justice."

He dizzily tried to back away from her but fell over in surprise and intoxication. His surroundings began to fade around him and he could only hear Sylvia say, "I don't want to do this, but I have to. It's my job."

He woke up after some time and found himself cuffed to a white table. He put his head down on the table to scratch his scalp. As he pulled his head up, Sylvia entered the room.

"Why did you bring me here?" he asked her in anger and confusion.

Answering his question with one of her own, Sylvia asked him, "Why did you lie to me about Michael Larry?"

Now even more confused, he asked her what she was talking about.

"Michael Larry died in San Quentin on the same day he arrived. He slit his own wrist and killed himself. Therefore, he could not have made that transaction, as he was already dead by then."

"But… but… but I assure you the account holder of that account went by the name Michael Larry, and… and I can prove it," Richard argued reluctantly.

Seconds later, the police chief walked in and wanted to join Sylvia in interrogating him. Then he realised that it was Richard 'Castle' King. He gasped and immediately went to his side and held his shoulders. He asked if he was indeed Richard King. Richard confirmed his thought and the police chief, in shock then asked, "**THE** Richard King?"

"The one and only," Richard responded arrogantly.

The police chief got very giddy and said, "Wow! I'm Mr Johnson. The chief of the NYPD. I am a **HUGE** fan of yours. I have *two* of each of your books."

Stupidly, he held out his hand to shake Richard's and

Richard looked down at the cuffs holding him to the table, to indicate to the police chief that he couldn't shake his hand while he was cuffed to the table.

"Oh, uhmm, quick... quick, cut him loose!" he yelled to Sylvia. "Oh, I am so sorry about this, Mr King," said the police chief as Sylvia released him from his cuffs.

"So, to what do I owe the pleasure of having **THE MR RICHARD 'CASTLE' KING** at our wonderful station?" asked the police chief, still giddy being in the presence of Richard.

"He is under arrest for lying to an officer of the law and attempting to defeat the ends of justice," Sylvia bluntly explained.

Richard, who was still rubbing his wrists after being let out of the cuffs, and the chief, who was about to drool over him, both turned to look at her.

"I've just told you, Sylvia, I have done no such thing," Richard said.

"No, no, no, no, no, Richard would do no such thing," the police chief agreed with him.

At that moment, the door opened, as Richard's mother, Yvonne, and his lawyer came in. The second Mr Johnson saw Richard's mother, he began to drool even more. "We-he-he-hell..." he said in a flirtatious tone, "what can I do for yyyyooooouuuu, madam?"

Richard and Sylvia stared at one another and slapped their foreheads in embarrassment at what was happening.

"You can let my son go, for starters, sir," Yvonne said to Mr Johnson bluntly.

Sylvia bluntly explained that they could do no such thing. That caused an argument to brew in that interrogation room, as Richard's lawyer argued that they could take him with them as he had not officially been charged. Richard's mother swung her handbag at Mr Johnson, who put his hand close to her waist and stared at her breasts through her dress. The four argued over separate matters, while Richard stood in the corner of the room with his hands folded and legs crossed, feeling embarrassed and waiting for them to get back to the matter that he was wrongfully arrested.

Five minutes later, a police officer, Mr Marston, walked in and said, "Detective Bec..." then froze in shock, seeing Sylvia and Richards's lawyer pushing and bumping each other with their breasts, and saw a woman beating up his boss with a handbag.

Upon his entry, they all froze and stared at him. Mr Johnson got up from the floor and put his hands on Yvonne again, then the silence was broken by the sound of the handbag impacting his face one last time, knocking him to the ground from which he didn't bother to stand up.

"Uhmm, De...tec...tive?" he said, still surprised and shocked.

"Yes?"

"Forensic report. Offshore account holder identified as a Mr Michael Larry."

Sylvia reached into her blouse and fixed her bra, which had moved around while bumping breasts with Richard's lawyer, and said "Oh, al...all... all right, Sergeant. You can leave now."

He awkwardly walked away, as everyone apart from Richard, fixed themselves up in the interrogation room. A few moments later, they all walked out of the room, apart from the police chief, and went outside. Sylvia apologised for the inconvenience that she had caused him and his mother drove him home.

Sylvia went to her desk and sat thinking about what the new evidence meant. Once Richard got home, he also decided to do the same, as he went to his laptop and typed a note to himself.

He knew the evidence meant one of two things. Either Michael Larry was alive and still operating his contract-killing agency, OR there was someone hiding behind his name and pretending to be him.

As the sun set, and shone a beautiful orange-purple light into his home office, he picked up his phone and called Sylvia. He asked her what exactly the case she was investigating was about. Feeling guilty about wrongfully arresting him, she told him that a man had been murdered in his mansion.

"Thirty-five-year-old male, shot clean in the back of his heart, found dead in the shower of his mansion. He was alone that week because his wife was away on a business trip. No witnesses and no tangible evidence was left behind. Our only current suspect seems too much of a coward to go through with such. We believed he was hired to kill our victim but now… we aren't so sure."

Upon hearing Sylvia say this to him, Richard laughed to himself and asked her, "Have you been reading my latest book?"

When she denied it, she stared down at the polished wood floor and said, "Then… why are you trying to sell me on the plot that I wrote in that book?"

The two, on opposite ends of the phone, both stood still, mesmerised by the thoughts going through their minds. The silence lasted so long that eventually they both hung up and went to think.

Sylvia left the station at the end of her shift and went directly to the local bookshop. As she walked up to it, she saw the banner outside with the words, *"Castle's newest novel now available!"*

and saw seven copies of his book in the store window. She bought a copy of Richard's book and went home. Richard at his penthouse went to his bedroom and lay on the bed... lost in wonder. He thought to himself, *"Did someone act on the plot I created, to take that man's life?"*

That night, in her bed, Sylvia lay in her black lingerie and read through Richard's book. As she read the chapter on the murder of his fictional victim, she realised a lot of consistencies between what he had written and the case she was working on.

The next day, she found herself at her desk, drinking her latte, when she caught sight of Richard going into Mr Johnson's office. A few minutes later, she found herself being summoned to his office.

"Ahh, Detective Beckette. You remember our friend, Mr King?"

She sarcastically replied, "How could I forget?"

Richard then explained to them that he believed that someone was taking his written plot and using it as a basis for the murder that they were currently investigating.

"You said you were a fan, Mr Johnson. Haven't you noticed the consistencies with my latest book?"

"Well, I haven't started reading it yet. But I bought it last week."

"It's true, sir, I bought his book last night and I noticed a lot of consistencies in what little I read."

"I didn't know you were one of my fans, Sylvia."

"I'm not, I just bought it for the sake of my investigation."

In the conversation, Richard asked a very important question to the investigators. "Have you questioned the wife yet?"

"Of course, spouses and family are always the first on the suspect list," Sylvia told him.

"And?"

"Her alibi checks out. She was three hundred miles away from the scene at the time of the crime."

Richard told them that he believed her to be the perpetrator.

"And what gives you that idea? You have never even met her," Sylvia asked, antagonising him.

"Could I see the crime scene?" Richard asked, with a grin of arrogance.

"Absolutely n—" Sylvia started.

"Of course. Anything for you, Mr King."

With the chief's agreement to his request, Sylvia slapped her forehead in disappointment. Mr Johnson would do anything for his attention. *"How pathetic,"* she thought to herself.

Richard and Sylvia went to her car and she drove them to the mansion that overlooked the coast. The trip was quiet. Neither of them said a word until they arrived.

Once they arrived, Richard looked around the mansion, with Sylvia bored by his apparent idiocy. He had no training of any sort, in this field. How could he possibly find something she hadn't found already?

"No forced entry?" Richard rhetorically commented.

"Yes, I know."

"So that means he knew whoever did this to him because only he and his wife would have had the key cards to access the building."

"Ha, no, the man had a household patroller and guards who had key cards too."

"Cards that would grant them access to the master bathroom?"

Sylvia looked at him in surprise and embarrassment. "How did I miss that?" she thought to herself.

While there were several people with key cards that would let them into the building, there were only two cards that could get them into the master bedroom and bathroom.

But then again, she had an alibi. One that could be verified. What a brainteaser.

Richard then looked at her and said, "Consider this. The wife could have left the house with her bags and gone to the airport where she bribed someone to make it seem like she was on the plane and landed safely three hundred miles away. Once she was informed that they had landed, she returned to the mansion and sneaked by the guards on duty. She would have known their exact positions as she lived in that very building and as such knew how the guards moved around. Once upstairs, scanned her key card and walked into the bathroom with a loaded gun. With his back turned to her, and unaware of her presence, she took aim at his most vital organ and pulled the trigger. She then made her escape as easily as she made her entrance and drove the three hundred miles to the hotel where she would stay and attend her business conference the very next day. She would have known that no matter what happened as she went through with his murder, she could explain it all away. Any hair or DNA she would have left behind would not be strong enough to convict her, as she lived in that very same mansion. She then returned when she was scheduled to, and '*discovered*' her dead husband. And while the police hunted a ghost who killed him, she drifted further off the radar and did what she does the best... disappear."

Intrigued by his theory, she thought of a response for him, but was interrupted by him, as he said, "I'm just saying, it makes a good story."

He walked across the glass floor that they were standing on and patted her shoulder twice as he walked downstairs.

While it was now obvious that everything he had just said was an idea for one of his future books, she had to admit to herself, it was a compelling theory and it made more sense than Richard probably noticed.

Her thoughts were interrupted as she heard him call out to her. "Sylvia!"

"Coming, Richard."

She walked down the stairs and Richard gazed at her as she sexily strutted her legs down the stairs, swaying her hips. He managed to control himself enough not to drool as she walked down to him.

They then walked outside to Sylvia's car, and she pulled out her phone and said, "Pick up the wife." And then hung up. Richard looked at her with a smile and got into her car. He stared at her, smiling, the whole way back to the station.

When they got there, Sylvia said, "Thanks for the angle, 'Castle'. That's your novelist name, right?"

"I thought you weren't a fan," he said, puzzled by why she was referring to him as Castle.

"I'm not. I saw it on the banner outside the bookshop last night."

He smiled at her, looked down and walked over to his car. He looked back at her as she said, "See you around, Richard."

Richard got into his car and said to himself, "You have no idea how right you are."

His plan was back on track. Well... partially. There was still more to be done but he was close to being able to execute his plan to try and win her heart.

Sylvia walked into the station and walked towards her desk. On her path, Marston speedily walked up beside her and told her that the wife was in the interrogation room. A wide grin went across her face and she changed her course, to head for the interrogation room.

"Mrs Watson. Remember me?"

"Of course. What do you want from me? I've already answered all your questions!"

"I'll get straight to the point. Did you kill your husband?"

"That... that... that's absurd. Of course, I didn't kill Cairo. I loved him with all my heart. Why on earth would I kill him?"

Sylvia looked deep into her eyes, trying to intimidate her. Though her tactic was futile, as her lawyer walked in and disrupted the interrogation. With no charges officially laid against her, Sylvia had no choice but to let her go. She had a very good suspect and a good angle on the case, but she knew that it was not enough. She had no apparent motive, nor was there any evidence against her. None that would be admissible in court at least, as Richard had said to her earlier in his thought, any trace of her, such as her DNA could be easily explained away, as she lived in the mansion. She needed more...

That night, as she put on her lingerie, she stared down at Richard's book, that she had bought the previous night. She never really planned to read the whole book but, on this night, with the smell of the moist grass coming through her bedroom window, she felt compelled to read it. She put on her reading glasses and read almost two chapters, lying in her bed. She eventually checked her phone, for the time, and seeing how late it was, she put the phone on 'Do Not Disturb', tucked it under her pillow and tried to fall asleep.

She woke up soon after midnight and stared up at the ceiling, thinking to herself. Richard had been so helpful in just the past few days; he might be able to help her put the whole case to bed. Especially since it seemed the perpetrator was a fan of his work, and he could therefore, likely, very easily get into this person's mindset.

She reached for her phone and, not even considering that he was most probably asleep, called Richard.

The pleasure in his voice when she answered the call was noticeable to Sylvia.

"My Detective Beckette, to what do I owe the pleasure of hearing your voice at this hour?"

"Still as flattering as ever, huh, 'Castle'? I wanted to ask if we could meet up for coffee tomorrow."

Richard rose to sit up in his bed. It was a pleasantly surprising request; however, he was curious as to why she would want to see him. Were his charms already working on her? He hadn't even begun with his grand, three-birds-with-one-stone plan.

"Are you asking me out?" he sarcastically commented.

She giggled sarcastically, in response and bluntly said, "Same place as before. Noon. Don't be late," and hung up.

The two then both lay back in their beds and tried to sleep. But, how could they? Sylvia had no clue how to ask him for his help when they went out, and Richard wondered what exactly she wanted. *Whatever it is, it must be important. Otherwise, she wouldn't call me this late,* he thought to himself.

Sylvia arrived at the coffee shop thirty minutes early for their meeting, hoping to get some time to practise her 'lines'. To her shock, as she walked in, there was Richard, waiting for her.

He stood up to pull out her chair for her, as a gentleman, and humorously commented on what she said to him at the end of their earlier call. "I'm not late."

"I can see that, Richard."

"So… to what do I owe this invitation?"

"Straight to the point, huh?"

"Indeed. I don't like beating around the bush."

Sylvia exhaled sharply and gave a slight giggle.

"You were kind of useful yesterday at the mansion."

"'Kind of'?" Richard asked, arrogantly.

"All right. VERY useful," she admitted. "And because of that, I would like your assistance in solving this entire case. I surmise it would be fairly easy for you to enter the perpetrator's mindset, as he OR she based their crime on the book you recently launched. So, will you help me?"

Richard smiled at her and laughed arrogantly.

"Of course. Anything for you, Sylvia," he said, flirtatiously.

It wasn't hard to see that he was flirting with her and she subtly told him off by saying, "You aren't doing this for me. You are doing it for the NYPD, and the family of our victim, Mr Watson."

The telling off hurt his ego slightly, but he now understood where he stood with her. He would still help her regardless. It would score him a few points before he kicked off his grand plan.

"Come with me then," Sylvia said, and the two walked outside to her car.

Chapter 3

They drove off and headed to the police station. Sylvia went to Mr Johnson and told him that Richard would be assisting her in her investigation, as they seemed to be dealing with someone who based this crime off the books Richard had written, and therefore he could likely enter the person's mindset fairly easily.

Mr Johnson agreed to let him work the case with her and they then went to her desk to get to work. Sylvia opened her laptop and started showing him the evidence that they had gathered. All of it was purely circumstantial, and pretty much inadmissible, in court.

As Richard looked through the evidence, he was very distracted and Sylvia noticed this.

"What's up?"

"Huh? Oh… oh… nah, it's nothing."

He downplayed the fact that he was distracted by her exquisite beauty and worked with her through the evidence file. Eventually, the sun had set and they had not found anything linking the wife to the case, nor any theories or made any progress of any sort.

Frustrated, Richard asked if she could copy the file to an external hard drive for him, so he could review the evidence at home. It went against the rules, but she did it anyway, because she knew that even if the boss found out, he wouldn't be angry since she was only giving the file to Richard.

Sylvia drove Richard to the coffee shop, where his car was

still sitting. The two then got in their separate cars and went to their respective homes.

Richard immediately went to pour himself a glass of Johnnie Walker whiskey and ordered some takeout for himself and his family. He played with his daughter, put her to sleep, and went to his bedroom.

"No ledgers or financial statement to draw up?"

"Not for a while. I'm on 'leave'."

"You have been on 'leave' for almost a week now."

"And your problem with that, Mother, is…?"

"You are never at home, you are getting wrongfully arrested, and you are on leave… What is going on with your life currently, my son?"

It was always very easy for his mother to see when something was wrong in his life, and this time was no different. Then again, his mother always was a little bit overbearing, and as such he did not want to tell her what was going on.

He downplayed his current problems and pretended to be drunk from the whiskey. His mother then left him in his room, alone, and went to bed.

Once he heard her snoring, he went to his office, plugged the external hard drive into his laptop and went through the evidence again.

He looked through it for hours and just as he felt like giving up… he hit pay-dirt.

Within the evidence file, there was the blueprint for the mansion. He compared it with the statements of the guards who were on duty that day. He looked through it thoroughly, trying to map the point where the perpetrator would have come in and made their exit while avoiding all the guards.

Through the main door… no, there was a guard right there.

Hmm... from the greenhouse, around the back... no, there would have been muddy impressions left in the dirt, and around the house. AGRRRRHHHH! he growled in frustration and then tried something different. He decided to work backward, from the bathroom, heading outwards.

Hmmm... well, the perpetrator would have had to go through the living room, up the stairs, past the vault, through the bedroom... WAIT! Past the vault?

He thought back to when he was in the mansion, he saw no vault when he went up and down the stairs.

Now, he had a lead. A very important clue. But he needed more. He needed more information. So, he dug into Mr Watson's information. He then discovered that Mr Watson used the same bank that he owned and worked for. That meant that he had access to all his financial records, dating back to when that account was first opened.

Looking way back to when he had the house built, he discovered that they bought a custom-made door with an RFID reader. He then had RFID tags baked into the two master key cards. The cards that only he and his wife had. Pieces were starting to fit together, and the wife looking guiltier and guiltier.

He grew more interested, as he scrolled through Mr Watson's financial records and discovered that he had purchased a large number of guns over the years. His curiosity was piqued and he was starting to develop a theory.

The next morning, he did the usual. Got up, showered, got dressed, ate breakfast and took his daughter to school. Afterwards, he immediately drove off to the station. He walked over to Sylvia with a huge smile on his face.

"Why so cheerful today?"

"'Cause I'm looking at your exquisitely beautiful face."

She looked down in worry that Richard was falling for her again. "Tell me, where are Mr Watson's belongings?"

"In the evidence room. Why?"

"I'd like to see something there."

"Well, unfortunately, authorised personnel only."

Sylvia soon found herself in the evidence room with Richard, regardless.

"I cannot believe how many rules I've already broken for you, Richard."

Richard looked through the box of evidence for Mr Watson's murder and found exactly what he was looking for at the very bottom. Mr Watson's key card.

He scanned it with his phone and cloned its frequency. His phone made a strange noise in the process and Sylvia grew sceptical.

"You better not be tampering with evidence, Richard, because if you are you will end up at the interrogation table again."

"Tampering... of course not. Come on. Trust me. Let's go back to the mansion."

"Again? For what?"

"You'll see when we get there. And I'm driving this time."

They got into his Benz and drove off to the mansion. Sylvia was bored and irritated by his request.

"I assure you; my team searched the entire house. All twenty-eight rooms. There won't be anything that we haven't found already," she told Richard as they walked through the mansion and headed up the staircase.

Richard then said to her, in a confident and sarcastic tone, "I think you mean twenty-nine rooms."

"Twenty-nine? No. What are you talking abo...?"

Confused, she followed Richard upstairs, now curious to know what he knew. As they reached the ninety-degree turn in the staircase, Richard stopped and pulled out his phone. Sylvia was now even more confused. He held his phone to a part of the wall, when they heard beeping and the sound of a lock moving. Then a large panel of the wall moved to reveal a secret room. The door blended in perfectly with the tiles of the wall, making it impossible to see.

"Have you checked in here?" Richard asked arrogantly.

She didn't bother answering him. She just pulled out her flashlight from inside her coat and went into the room, followed by Richard. The second they walked in, lights automatically turned on, and there, in that room was the biggest piece of the puzzle. Mr Watson's extensive gun collection. Rifles, pistols, shotguns, every last gun he had collected over the years.

"Whoa!" Sylvia exclaimed in amazement. "H…ho…how did you know about this room?" she asked Richard.

"Blueprints," he answered arrogantly.

Sylvia wanted to slap herself on the forehead again. How did she miss that?

"Now, aside from the architect and builders of this mansion, there are only two people who knew about this room. Mr and Mrs Watson," Richard explained to Sylvia as she pulled her phone out and made a call ordering for officers to come and take all the weapons for testing.

As they wandered the room, Richard noticed something. A small pistol. It stood out from all the others because it lay in a glass case, all by itself. Below it, there was a gold plaque beneath its case that read, "Smith and Wesson Model four-ten"

The thing that stood out most was the pink impression on the red cushion it sat on. It appeared to show where the gun usually lay. The gun also was crooked, unlike all the other weapons that lay perfectly straight. It was clear that the gun had been moved recently. Which seemed odd.

Sylvia and Richard looked at each other with a knowing look in their eyes. They said, *That's the murder weapon* to one another in their heads.

Once the police arrived, Sylvia ordered all the guns to be taken for forensic analysis, and ballistics comparison to the bullet retrieved from Mr Watson's heart.

They left and Sylvia looked at Richard with a keen eye. She was impressed by his powers of deductive logic. He drove her back to the station and told her to call him when the results were in.

"Aren't you going to stay for the rest of the day?"

"No. I have to go make notes about this. For my next book."

"It's kind of your book's fault that this seemingly innocent man died."

Richard shrugged his shoulders, shut his door and drove off. He got home and typed a note to himself.

'*My first case. What an experience it has been. Today, we might have found the main piece of the puzzle. Me and my Sylvia. Well, I hope to make her mine soon enough, at least. She rocks my world. Now to execute my grand plan... just as soon as this case is solved. I suppose I'm back in the game. The game of love. I've been out of this game for so long. In fact, the last time I played, was with this same woman, Sylvia. There was, of course, that slut who gave me my adorable first child but... that wasn't love. It was just sex. To me... But I'll say this. It kind of feels good being back in the game.*'

His pre-game try-out was almost complete. All he needed to do was wait for this case to be put to bed, and he could execute his grand plan...

Three days later, around eight o'clock in the morning, he received a call from Sylvia.

"You need to come down to the station. Now!"

He was surprised, so he went to the elevator, jumped into his car and drove off to the station. When he arrived, Sylvia was standing at the entrance. He smiled out of his curiosity and flirtatiously said, "I knew you couldn't stay away from me." Sylvia just gave a gentle scoff and pointed her index finger in his direction and curled it towards herself several times, as if to say, "Follow me." She then led him to her desk and handed him a thick document.

"Second paragraph, last sentence. Read it," Sylvia instructed Richard, with a bright grin on her face. *"...ballistics tests show that the bullet marking left on the bullet found in the victim's heart is a perfect match to the bullets test fired from the Smith and Wesson model 410 found in the victim's gun collection."*

Richard realised that he was holding the forensic report. He smiled and stared into Sylvia's eyes, with pride and satisfaction. They found their killer, and the evidence they needed to convict her. They stared into each other's eyes for several minutes, and only stopped when they heard the station doors being opened with force. There, being brought into the station in handcuffs, was their killer, Mrs Watson.

"Shall we?" Richard rhetorically asked Sylvia, pointing out his hand, in the direction of the interrogation room. Sylvia only smiled and walked to the interrogation room, with Richard right behind her.

"Mrs Watson. Nice to see you again," Sylvia said

sarcastically.

"My lawyer will sue the skirt off you for this harassment! I have already told you I had nothing to do with my Cairo's death! And… who's your boyfriend over here?" she replied in anger and Sylvia and Richard stared at each other, then back at her.

"This is Mr Richard King. He has been assisting me on your husband's case."

"Richard King?"

"Yes."

"The novelist?"

She burst out laughing, and asked in an insulting manner, "What did you need him for? To scratch under your breasts? That's probably the only place he could find 'evidence'."

She continued laughing out loud while Richard looked at her, feeling angry, and asked, "What do you mean by that, madam?"

Sylvia stood up for him, and said to Mrs Watson, "He has been very useful. He helped to uncover details about your husband that even *you* failed to mention to me."

Mrs Watson immediately stopped laughing and asked Detective Beckette what she was talking about.

"Your husband's gun collection, for instance," Sylvia pointed out to her.

Instantly her demeanour changed. Trying to throw them off, she asked, "What gun collection?"

"The one we found in a hidden room, along the staircase of your home."

Mrs Watson swallowed hard and looked down at the table.

"So, care to tell me what happened that day, Mrs Watson?"

"I think I'm going to wait for my lawyer."

"Well, just know that the police are going through your hotel room as we speak. Lawyer or no lawyer."

Mrs Watson looked at them in fear and turned to look away from them. Her lawyer was in court with another client so it would be a while before she arrived. The police who had gone to raid her room got back to the station and went to the interrogation room.

"Detective. We found a bullet casing among her belongings. It's soaked in blood."

Sylvia's smile grew wider and she ordered them to send it to the forensics lab, for testing. She then turned to face Richard with a smile, and he smiled back at her.

"So… care to explain that, Mrs Watson?"

She paused and then said, "I'm going to give you one last chance to tell me the true story, ma'am."

"No need. I can do that for you, Sylvia," Richard said, interrupting them. He looked over to Mrs Watson, who was avoiding eye contact, and began to tell them the sequence of events that occurred in Mr Cairo Watson's last hours alive.

"So, you left the house, and headed off, in your car, to the airport to catch your plane. You then somehow got your luggage on the plane and arranged to have it picked up by someone at the hotel where you were going to stay, making it seem like you were on the plane while you actually stayed behind. You then drove back to the house and entered through your garage, as you knew there would be no guard at your garage, since your car was not there. Going through the garage you went through the house and up the stairs, avoiding all the interior guards. You then used your master key card to get into the vault where Cairo stored his gun collection and took out the gun which you knew was his favourite, the Smith and Wesson model 410, to kill him with it. You then used your master key card to get into the master bedroom, where you expected to find him. That's when you realised, he was in the shower, with his music on. You swiped your key card to get in and took aim, for his heart, while he was unaware of your presence, and pulled the trigger. When your naked husband fell to the floor, you went over to him to pick up the bullet and casing of the single round you had fired into his heart. You then realised the bullet was lodged in his heart, and you couldn't take it out. So, you picked up the casing that was now soaked in the blood pouring out of your husband's wound and kept it as a trophy. You took the gun back and put it among his collection, where it belonged, but did not place it properly, which exposed the pattern of where the gun had sat for an extended period of time, showing it had recently been moved. You then snuck back outside, got in your car and made the trip to the hotel you were meant to be staying in, and peacefully went to sleep, to prepare for your conference the next day. Correct?"

Mrs Watson looked up at the two of them and nodded, so as to indicate that, blow by blow, Richard had the story correct.

Sylvia looked beside her, over to Richard, and asked, "How did you figure that out? The guard and garage thing, I mean?"

"The guards only guard the garages when the cars are parked in them. Since her car was not in the garage, the guard was off duty. The other garage guard was guarding the garage on the other side of the house, where Cairo's car was parked. He could not have seen her from there."

"How did you find that out?"

"I checked the guard schedules and contracts, which clearly describe every detail of the guard's duties. This included."

Sylvia looked over to Mrs Watson and shook her head.

"Okay, but then how come none of the guards heard the gunshot?" she asked Mrs Watson. Richard interrupted and answered that too.

"That room is soundproof."

"How do you know that?"

"Transaction made to a home improvements company, three years ago, shows that they had the master bedroom and bathroom soundproofed."

Sylvia, shocked by the information she had missed and Richard had collected, looked down at the floor and then up at Mrs Watson.

"Is this true?"

Mrs Watson, ashamed that she had been caught out, looked up to Sylvia and nodded, confirming what Richard had just said.

"Yes. You see, my husband was a sex addict, so we had sex almost every day, in the bed at night and in the shower, because his erection was strongest when we had sex in the shower, I think because then my breasts and vagina were more exposed for him to see, as opposed to when we were in the blankets and he could only feel my 'bubbles' and… etcetera. Now since we had sex so much, the guards and visitors always complained about the loud, 'passionate' noises coming from the shower and bedroom, so we had those two rooms soundproofed so that people couldn't hear when we were having sex."

The explanation for the soundproofed rooms was a bit… 'too detailed', but it made sense and helped to further explain the case.

"All right. I have one last question for you then, Mrs Watson. Why did you do it?"

Mrs Watson exhaled and looked down at the table that she was cuffed to.

"My father is unwell. The surgery and operations that he needs to have done are very expensive. Now my dad and Cairo never really got along, and so Cairo refused to pay for them. So, we needed money. I had been sending almost my whole salary home over the past few months and it did not even cover twenty-five per cent of the costs. So, I needed the money. So, I dec—"

Richard then interrupted her, with an understanding of what was going through her mind at the time, and finished her sentence with what he figured she was about to say.

"So, you decided to kill him and try to cash in on his life insurance policy?" Richard asked.

In shame, she exhaled heavily and replied, "Yes. But... little did I know, he had listed the beneficiary of his life insurance money as Zoey Watson. Our daughter. He also left all his assets, the mansion, his cars, his businesses, EVERYTHING to Zoey. Now she never liked her grandfather either, and she also refuses to pay for his medical requirements. Instead, she spent all his life insurance money on the funeral, because she wanted him to have the most dignified funeral possible, as she always loved her dad more than me. As for the rest of what she has inherited, she still doesn't know what to do with it all, but helping my father is near the bottom of her priority list."

"So basically, you got nothing out of this crime?" Sylvia asked her antagonistically. Mrs Watson was too ashamed to say anything, so she just nodded once and looked away.

She had practically pleaded guilty to the murder of her husband and couldn't undo that. When her lawyer finally arrived, she could do nothing for her. The charges had been laid and she had pled guilty. All that really lay ahead of her was the trail and a cell.

Officers came to put her in her cell, and Richard and Sylvia walked outside. They stood side by side and faced forward to the sunset. They then looked at each other and smiled as they separated and went to their cars and drove to their separate homes.

Later that evening, Richard sat at his office desk, typing an 'improved' version of the case he and Sylvia had put to rest. While he was working, his daughter came to him and soothed his spirit, with a short chat. She then gave him a goodnight kiss on the cheek and went to bed. Richard sat still thinking for a moment how he and the now-deceased Cairo Watson had something in common. They both had daughters whom they loved dearly and their daughters both loved their fathers more than their mothers.

He then started typing a note to himself.

'Cairo's case has been solved. It feels satisfying. Though yet at the same time, it feels a little bit sad. Mrs Watson, who has now pleaded guilty to her husband's murder, will stand trial in a month. I can't wait.

Once she is behind bars... I will be able to execute my grand plan. The plan that will help me kill three birds with one stone. I will get all three things I want... a brilliant plot for my next best seller... the pleasure of helping to make my city a better and safer place... and most importantly... the woman of my dreams, Sylvia Beckette.'

Meanwhile, on the other side of the city, Sylvia took off her clothes and feeling that she wanted to have sex that night, acted like a stripper for herself in front of the mirror, until she was naked. She then decided to put on her navy lingerie, to take a break from her black one that she had worn for a while. She then looked down at Richard's book which she had been reading a little bit of every night since she bought it. She had to admit it was a very good book. She couldn't believe it but maybe, just maybe, she was turning into one of Richard 'Castle' King's fans.

That felt odd to admit. Even to herself.

When she decided to stop reading for that night, she turned her phone off, put it on her wireless charging pad, took off and folded her glasses, lay them beside her bed light and went to sleep.

Still in the mood to have sex that night, she held her breasts and flicked her nipples, to try and fool herself into thinking a guy was playing with them while sleeping with her. Then, she stopped and looked up. A thought crossed her mind. What would it be like to kill someone you had sex with almost every day? The thought ruined her mood, and she rolled over to fall asleep.

The next morning, they went back to their normal routines. Richard went to his office at the bank, of which he was the majority owner, and got back to ledgers and statements. Sylvia, to her detective desk to put together the case file for the trial of Mrs Watson.

They both were distracted that day. Richard missed Sylvia. The love of his life. Seeing her practically every day for the past fortnight or so gave him great pleasure. Sylvia also missed Richard. She had enjoyed working with him recently and she honestly enjoyed his simultaneous personality of a foolish flirt and a genuine genius.

Eventually, after what seemed an eternity, Richard woke up to the sound of his virtual assistant, Bixby, alerting him there was something important to do that day. Finally... it was time for Mrs Watson's trial. After only five hours of hearing the evidence, the jury went to deliberate. The deliberation lasted only two hours, and Mrs Watson was found guilty of first-degree murder. Her sentence was a minimum of fifty years in prison, being eligible for parole once she had completed half her sentence. To everyone in that courtroom, justice had been served.

Sylvia went to the balcony on the highest floor and stared at the sun as it set on that day. She was satisfied, and proud to have performed her civic duty, by putting another dangerous person behind bars. She heard footsteps coming up behind her on the concrete floor. She didn't even have to turn around to figure out who it was.

"So, we did it, huh?"

"That we did, Richard. And on behalf of the NYPD, thank you for all your help."

"It was only a pleasure."

He put his hand over hers and they stared on at the sunset together.

"Would you like to grab some dinner?" Richard asked Sylvia.

She turned to face him and smiled. "Sure. Why not? But you are buying, 'Castle'."

She turned and pulled his arm, giggling to herself. They walked to their cars and drove off to a nearby five-star restaurant, where they ate high-class food and drank French wine.

"To a safer city," Sylvia toasted.

"To a safer city," Richard toasted as they drank and laughed together. They sat together until the restaurant manager came to tell them that they were about to close. Richard paid the bill and they went outside.

They each got into their cars and spoke through the windows. "Have yourself a splendid evening Ms Beckette."

"You too, Mr King."

Sylvia started her engine and said, "I'll see you around Richard." then reversed and drove off. Richard, left alone in the parking area of the restaurant, giggled to himself, put his head on the steering wheel then rose with a deep inhale. He said to himself, "You have no idea, Sylvia," then started the engine and drove home.

He got back to find that both his mother and daughter were asleep. He went to his trophy cabinet and stared at his certificates and copies of his books. He thought to himself, all that success... it always meant the most to him but... Sylvia would mean more to him than all of them combined.

He then went into his room, took off his suit and lay on the bed in his boxers, with one arm under his head. Looking up, he whispered to himself, "Tomorrow, we put our GRAND plan into action..."

He then dozed off and fell asleep, impatient for the rising of the sun.

Chapter 4

The next morning, Richard was woken up by the bright orange light of the sunrise shining through his curtains. For that moment, every aspect of the world seemed to be in perfect harmony. Until his alarm buzzed, letting him know that it was seven o'clock. And so, with that he got ready to execute his master plan.

He went to the bathroom, showered, brushed his teeth, and went to get dressed. As he stood in front of his mirror, in his boxers, he smiled with confidence. "Here it goes," he whispered to himself. He jumped into his pants, threw his shirt on, buckled his belt, fastened his tie, jumped into his beige loafers and threw on his jacket, all with great precision and confidence. He picked up a banana from the fruit bowl in the kitchen and went to his car. He hopped in and drove off for the police station.

When he arrived and stuck his foot out the car, to stand up, he was so confident that everything around him seemed to be going in slow motion. It was the fact he was just moving slowly on purpose to look 'cool' and show his confidence. He shut the car door and walked towards to police station entrance, with his wavy locks flowing in the morning breeze. People looked at him and hid their faces as they laughed at him, looking ridiculous, walking in slow-motion.

Once inside, he strutted his walk, now a bit faster than outside, so as not to embarrass himself and he headed straight for the police chief's office. He didn't even knock, he just walked in, and said, with great confidence, "We need to ta—"

He interrupted himself, when he realised that Mr Johnson was on the phone and he was talking hyper sexually with... whoever was on the other side of the phone. All he heard was, "I hope your boobs are still as bubbly as I remem..." and that's when the silence came.

Mr Johnson then said, "Uhhhhmmm, listen, I'll see you later, doll face. I have to go." He then whispered into phone, "Hey, put on the panther look tonight." There was silence for a moment but he still didn't drop the phone. A few seconds later, he whispered, "Of course with all four of your bubbles out." He couldn't whisper soft enough however and Richard overheard every word. Looking to his side and now feeling very awkward, Richard waited for him to drop the call. Mr Johnson then laughed and said, "You are so nasty." Still trying to whisper but not succeeding at preventing Richard from hearing. Mr Johnson then looked at Richard, who was now very awkward, and quickly said, "Okay, bye-bye."

"I'm sorry to interrupt," Richard said, and Mr Johnson excused him.

"So, what can I do for my favourite novelist?"

"Permission to be frank?"

"Granted."

"I'd like to work with your homicide detective for a while. I need a few good ideas for my next book and I have been struggling to find anything interesting. I do not want my readers to get bored with my pieces."

Mr Johnson looked up at him and told him that it was not something he could easily agree to, since he may get hurt. Then Richard played his trump card.

"You already know I can handle myself, Mr Johnson. I've already helped solve a big case. In fact, I found all the convicting evidence that your officers missed," Richard said, arrogantly.

"That you have. And I would love to help you, as you know, I'm a fan of yours... All right then. I can let you work alongside Detective Beckette for a two-month period."

"That should be perfect."

"Well then... welcome to the NYPD."

"Thanks, but I'm not joining the force, I'm just doing research."

"One is as good as another."

"All right then well, thank you, Mr Johnson."

"It's Benjamin. Or Ben. At least to you..."

He stopped their conversation by ringing his intercom buzzer, which made a loud buzz as it amplified his voice, to summon Sylvia to his office.

When Sylvia entered his office, she was surprised to see Richard.

"Meet your new partner."

"My new partner? Richard? Wha... Huh?"

The look on Sylvia's face was priceless. She argued that he couldn't be her partner, since he had no police training or anything of the sort.

Richard then explained to her that he was not her 'partner' partner, he was just going to be working on cases with her as research for his next book.

Sylvia exhaled heavily and realised that Richard had exploited Mr Johnson's fandom of him to get him to agree to this.

She then tried to act as if she cared about Richard's safety, and argued that he could get hurt. They easily dismissed that and Mr Johnson told her it would only be for two months. He then sent them out of his office. Sylvia, forced to go along with this, then gave him a lowdown on how it would work. Simple things, but so many that it gave him a mini-migraine.

Richard then went home and told Sylvia to call him when there was a case for them to work. Sylvia did not expect it to be too soon, which would give her time to think of a way to get rid of him. She wasn't really worried that he would get in her way or anything along those lines. She was worried that feelings would surface from one of them, and she was too afraid of that happening.

The very next morning she was in the shower when the phone rang. She knew, by the ringtone that went off, it was the PD. She ran out of the shower naked to answer the phone. There was a homicide...

She finished her shower and called Richard to tell him.

"We've got a case. Come to Central Park. Now."

"Who was murdered?"

His question was not even answered, as she hung up before he finished asking.

Twenty minutes later, they were in Central Park. There was a moat that surrounded a flower garden. There, in the moat, was a small row boat, surrounded by crime scene investigation tape. A young man lay in that boat. Dead.

It was not hard to see that the guy did not die there.

"Guy identified as a Mr Brian Walker. Seems he was shot with a high calibre revolver. Time of death approximately one-thirty AM."

It seemed to be very violent, almost professional, until Richard said something.

"Killed by someone he knew. Probably a first-time killer."

"What makes you think that, Richard?"

"If it was someone experienced, they'd have just throw his body in the water, and any evidence would have been washed away."

Sylvia felt pretty stupid when he said that. It was like a boss being outsmarted by his intern.

"Also, where he was shot shows this crime was taken out on him by someone he knew."

Surely enough, Sylvia could not dispute that. Brian had been shot in his penis and bled to death from there. If you just wanted him dead for no reason, you'd have shot him in the head or the heart. And there was something else.

"Seems the killer took a trophy from him too," Sophia, the medical examiner, announced to Sylvia and Richard.

"Why do you say that?" Sylvia asked in surprise.

"He's only got one testicle."

That thought was disgusting to everyone. Who kills someone and then keeps one of their testicles?

"I'll give you guys a full briefing down at the lab, after the full autopsy." said Jessica, the examiner.

Sylvia and Richard looked and decided to walk around the park with the crime scene investigators, trying to find any other evidence. It did not take very long for them to find a large round mark in the grass of the park. It looked like mud, but it was actually blood. They gathered some up and sent it for testing. Also, in the fish pond, just one hundred yards from where the body was found, they found Brian's missing testicle.

"What a case this is going to be."

"You can say that again. Come on. We have to go talk to Brain's parents."

"Why?"

"Family are always the first suspects. Lesson one, Richard."

"I really do not see any parent shooting their son in his manhood and pulling out one of his balls, then dumping him in boat to just float away."

"Me neither. But it has to be done."

They got into Sylvia's car and drove off to where his parents lived. They were devastated by the news that their only son was dead. They could not think of any reason as to why someone would want him dead.

Richard and Sylvia then left and went to the station for the autopsy results.

There was almost no evidence on him, beside the visible evidence they had gathered from the crime scene. They had no DNA evidence. No apparent motive. Nothing useful.

"This is the worst way to start an investigation, because then everyone is a suspect." Sylvia told her new 'partner'.

"Everyone?"

"Everyone..."

"Okay, I call dibs on interrogating you then," Richard said humorously.

Sylvia smiled at the stupidity of his remark.

"Come on. We're going to the kid's school," Sylvia told him.

Upon their arrival at the school, it was very quiet as the students mourned their fellow learner. All the teachers and the principal could only speak highly of Brian. No suspects emerged from there.

Back at the station, they scratched their heads, searching for something to point them to a suspect. At the same time, someone was also impatient for the killer to be caught, and this person knew who the killer was.

Sylvia's phone rang and she answered to be greeted by a much-distorted voice.

"Beckette."

"Detective. I know who killed Brian Walker."

"Who is this?"

"That's not important."

"Uhmm... yes, it i—"

"His name is Ronald Phillips. He was Brian's dealer, until the deal went sour. Good luck, he's a slippery little guy."

"Wait, how do you kn—hello? HELLO?"

That conversation ended then and there. Sylvia looked up at Richard with a smile as bright as sunlight. She ordered her men to find this Ronald fellow, and took Richard with her to confront Brian's parents.

Mr and Mrs Walker were still in tears, just as Richard and Sylvia had left them. It felt wrong to confront them while they were still grief struck, but it had to be done.

"Did you know your son was involved in drugs?" Detective Beckette asked them. The look on their faces as her question hit their ears was curious.

They admitted that they knew that he was involved in drugs, but they did not tell anyone because it would taint their image even more after the law suit, they had just lost.

"So, it did not occur to you to tell us earlier? I mean, his dealer would have made a perfect first suspect, if Brian had not paid him recently."

"Dealer?"

"Yes."

"Brian did not have a dealer, Detective..."

"I thought you said he was involved in drugs?"

"He was."

"How did he get drugs if he had no dealer, then?"

"He did not get drugs. He SOLD drugs. He was the drug dealer."

There was a long pause of silence as Sylvia processed the

thought portrayed by this new information.

"What?"

"Yes. He dealt drugs, through his five best buddies."

"Best buddies?"

"Yeah. Nicole, Jim, Ross, Angelo and Michelle.

This conversation shocked both Richard and Sylvia. Everyone they had spoken to said Brian was a little angel, and now he was a drug kingpin...

They left and went back to the station where Ronald had been arrested and was waiting to be interrogated. Sylvia and Richard went in and tried to make the interrogation as quick as smooth as possible.

"Do you know why you are here, Mr Phillips?"

"Yeah, I think so. It must be about Brian."

"Right, so let's make this easy. Did you kill him?"

"Kill... wait... what?"

"Did you kill Brian Walker?"

"What are you guys talking about? Is... is... is Brian dead?" Sylvia and Richard looked across at each other.

"Did you not just tell Detective Beckette and me that you thought that this was about Brian?" Richard asked in the attempt to contradict Ronald.

"I thought Brian had snitched on me for dealing drugs to him..."

"I thought Brian was the drug dealer?"

"Yeah, he was. He dealt the drugs that I sold him. I was his supplier." Sylvia then took back the interrogation from Richard.

"Do you realise that you have just confessed to a crime."

"...yes..."

"When last did you see Brian?"

"Last night."

"Where?"

"In Central Park."

"What where you guys doing there?"

"I was giving him his weekly package."

"Drug package?"

"Yeah. His and his friends'."

"Friends?"

"Yeah, Ross, Nicole and… I could never remember the other three's names."

"Jim, Michelle and Angelo?"

"Yes! Them! How did you know?"

Richard and Sylvia looked across to each other again. Smiling. But for different reasons.

They ended the interrogation then and there. When they went to the kitchen, they agreed that they needed to talk to these five buddies of Brian's. They had been mentioned twice in one day, in one case.

Sylvia then explained to Richard that they needed their story to convict Ronald.

"Convict him?"

"Yes. Eye witness accounts and he goes to jail for a long time."

"You don't think maybe they have something to do with this?"

"Why? We already have a suspect, who has placed himself with the victim, at the crime scene and has confessed to being involved in a crime with Brian. What more do we need?"

Richard had always had a strong gut, and his was telling him, *'The dealer was there, but he didn't have anything to do with this.'*

When they returned to the school that Brian and his friends

attended, they found the five of them on the football field, mourning the loss of their friend, Brian.

Sylvia's wish came true. They confirmed Ronald being there, and told him what she was already assuming. Brian was buying drugs off Ronald to sell, but he owed him money, for previous deliveries. He did not have it though, because he used all his money on alcohol, as of recent. They asked if one of them could identify the dealer from a photo line-up.

They all volunteered. All but one of them, choose Ronald's face. The fifth, Nicole, choose none of them.

That was very strange, but hey had enough to convict Ronald now. And everyone, except Richard, was satisfied. Something did not make sense to him, but he couldn't figure out what.

Richard soon went home. He had ideas to jot down, and a long day to process and sleep off. As he sat at his desk after dinner, his mother walked into his office and asked, "How was the first day on the job?"

Richard looked at her puzzled. "How…"

"Oh, that Ben. He's been calling me, none stop, and he told me. So, I've got a writer, accountant and detective all in one son?"

"I guess."

"How was the first case?"

"Short if anything is to be said."

"Wow! How rare."

"What?"

"Murder cases are usually pretty long. Maybe it's because of your books."

She kissed Richard's cheek and left him be as she went to bed. Richard giggled to himself and then looked up.

"Murder cases are usually pretty long…"

Of course! He immediately called Sylvia and pointed it out to her. "Why did this case go by so quickly?"

"Because of the tip off, I guess."

"Exactly! Why were we tipped off before the case even became public knowledge?"

Sylvia sprung up from her bed in thought. She had to admit it to herself, this case was too easy. It was clear that whoever called in knew too much to be a random civilian. And why was the voice scrambled? In New York, you want the world to see your face when you help the police solve a case, especially murder.

"We'll talk more in the morning, Richard," Sylvia said and hung up. She now had on sleep with a huge question on her mind.

The next morning Sylvia arrived at her desk to find Richard already waiting for her. She openly admitted that Richards point made a lot of sense. Things happened too easily. They needed to find out why.

Richard pointed out the two things that needed investigating. First of all, who was the person behind the distorted voice with the tip off? And secondly, why did Nicole not choose Ronald in the photo line-up.

They had a trace run on the call however that attempt was futile. The call signal was bounced though several other phones and then buried with a micro router.

"One thing is for sure, whoever tipped us off about all this is very rich." Richard pointed out to them, and they all agreed.

Thirty minutes later they were at the home of Mr and Mrs Bandeira. Nicole's parents. They questioned Nicole on why she did not identify Ronald as Brian's drug supplier.

"You guys asked for his drug supplier. It was none of those guys."

"Then how come all your friends pointed this guy… out as his supplier in the line-up?" Sylvia asked as she drew his photo from her case file.

Nicole looked at the face and then up to them.

"This is my ex-boyfriend."

Silence struck and confusion began to brew in Sylvia and Richards minds.

"What?"

"This is my ex. He didn't supply Brian. Brian supplied him."

"So why does everyone believe it was the other way around?"

"Because Ronald was once his suppler until Brian took over his cartel."

"And when was this?"

"Shortly after we broke up."

"How do you know?"

"I convinced Brian to take it over because Ronald was too slow on supplying the six of us."

"You, Brian and your friends?"

"Yes."

Now the supposedly simple case was getting more and more complex. And more confusing.

"Why did you not tell us this?"

"Because…"

She couldn't finish her sentence. She broke down and cried in her mother's arms. Sylvia couldn't ask her anything in her distraught state and so she and Richard left. As they headed for the door Richard said a very cliché thing as he walked.

"Don't leave town."

They left and went back to the police station to talk to Ronald who was still in custody. They explained what Nicole had told them and Ronald confirmed it.

"So why exactly where you meeting at central park that night?"

"I wanted to buy from him for my cousin. That's when I my ex, Nicole, saw me and I decided to leave without them…"

"You keep confessing to more and more crimes as you try you explain your way out of murdering Brian."

"I DID NOT KILL BRIAN!"

"Then why does everyone think you did?"

"Because… they think I wanted my cartel back."

"And you didn't?"

"No. I wanted to go straight. That's why I *gave* Brian my cartel."

"You gave it to him?"

"Yes."

Now the case against Ronald was crumbling. They now had no motive or anything. All they had was him with the victim, but according to him he was still alive when he left. With no solid evidence left to convict Ronald… they had no choice but to let him go.

Richard sat with Sylvia at her desk trying to figure out what angle to explore next when Sylvia's phone rang.

"Beckette."

"Detective. Why did you let Ronald go?"

Sylvia's eyes open wide. It was the distorted voice again.

"Because he is innocent."

"You are a fool to believe that. He may not have pulled the trigger but he planned out the whole thing."

"How do you know all this, sir? Or ma'am?"

"Sir. And I know because he paid me to do it."

"To kill Brian?"

"No, to put his plan in place. Never mind, I'll send you something in a little while and you'll understand."

Beckette told Richard what had just happened and her phone beeped seconds later. The mysterious voice had sent her a photo of a document. A document with instructions to plant a bullet in a gun, the location of the gun and where to dispose of it.

Then the phone rang again. Sylvia did not even have to confirm who she was talking to. It was the encrypted voice.

"Got it now?"

Sylvia wanting full clarity on what happened replied, "No." The person grew impatient and began to explain.

"Ronald had a revolver that he and Nicole used to play with whenever they had sex because they both loved police roll-play. He hid the gun for me to find and instructed me to load it and swap it with a gun that Ross owned."

"And then...?"

"You can figure the rest out yourself detective." The caller hung up.

"Come on, let's go."

"Where are we going?"

"To where those plans instruct to dispose of the weapon, Richard."

Richard, still with his gut whispering to him that something was not right, got up and went with her.

Just as the plans had shown, there was a revolver buried in a field just beyond New York City.

Later the police had run a search on the serial number. The gun was indeed registered to Ronald Phillips.

"Before we go pick him up, let's go talk to Ross," Richard said to Sylvia.

"Why?"

"We need to know how he is connected to all of this."

"What do you mean? He was the victim's friend."

"How does a high school child obtain ownership of a gun? And how did our 'informant' and Ronald know about it?"

Sylvia stood silently and eventually said, "I think we should go talk to Ross."

"Now why didn't I think of that?" Richard said sarcastically as they went down to the underground parking lot to go and visit Ross Lappin.

Chapter 5

When Richard and Sylvia arrived at Ross's house, something was clearly wrong with him. He was shaking, sweating... obviously nervous.

"Where'd you get the gun?"

"Gun?"

"We have information that you own a gun."

"No. I don't have a gun. My father does."

"Have you ever used it?"

"Which one?"

"I thought you just said your dad has a gun?"

"He has about twenty. He's a collector."

At that moment, Ross's parents came home from work. They were surprised to find Ross with two strangers, in their house.

"Who are you?"

"Detective Richard King and Sylvia Beckette," Richard answered.

"Detective Beckette and... writer Richard King," Sylvia corrected.

They explained to the couple that they believed Ross was involved in the murder of his friend Brian, and that they now suspected that Ross used one of his father's guns to commit the crime.

"That's impossible," Ross's dad argued.

"How do you know?"

"Because I am the only one who can get into the vault with

my gun collection."

"With what? A key card?" Richard asked sarcastically.

Ross's dad then took his phone's flashlight and shone the light on his hand, where a purple light seemed to glow from within his hand.

"What is that?" Beckette asked in awe.

"It's and RFID implant. It's the only way in or out of the vault."

"So, have you checked your collection recently?"

"Every morning."

"Is anything missing?"

"No."

Sylvia and Richard looked across at each other and then, suddenly, Ross broke down into tears. At that moment, Ross's parents asked Richard and Sylvia to leave. They went back to the station and headed their separate ways to their homes.

Richard got home and had his dinner and spent some quality time with his daughter. He then tried to go to sleep. However, that particular night he couldn't. He walked up and down the penthouse and eventually decided to go out for a drive. He did not have any specific destination but he found himself back at the police station. He went in through the underground parking and went to Sylvia's desk. (The desk they practically shared.)

He took the case file and started scouring through it. That's when something hit him. There was one detail that everyone, himself included, had forgotten. Brian had been shot in his penis, and his testicle taken and thrown in a nearby fish pond.

That was not a typical way to kill someone. Especially with the motives that Ronald had. It meant that the killer was likely someone who had a sexual fetish over Brian. Things did not seem to make very much sense now. With every possible answer that they got, it seemed that more questions came up. None the less he needed to remind Sylvia of this. This was their biggest clue of all. So, he decided to wait there for her to arrive the next morning. Inadvertently he fell asleep.

When Sylvia arrived in the morning, she was surprised and slightly embarrassed to find Richard in her chair, fast asleep, still in his boxers and vest. She did not want the other officers to see him like this and she drew back her right thigh and prepared to kick him to wake him up.

Before she released the kick, she noticed the shape created in the centre of his boxers by his erect penis, which she then could judge was a big penis. A memory then played in her mind to something she and a few of her friends had discussed in St 6. *'Why is it that all girls wake up with a yawn and all boys wake up erect?'*

Probably because of their love for sex, she answered to herself in her head. That's when she felt something deep inside her. Not only was she now in the mood to have sex, but she realised something. Their victim, Brian, was shot in his genitals and his testicle taken and thrown away. She now had the same concept for the killer that Richard had been waiting to tell her.

She let loose the kick and launched Richard out of the chair and woke him up.

"Get up, 'Castle'!"

He shuffled on the ground and tried to stand up, scared and confused, he exclaimed with saliva falling from his mouth like a fountain.

"Hu...! Wha...?"

"You can't sleep here. Nor can you be here dressed like that. Go home and get dressed."

"Morning to you too, Sylvia. How did you sleep?"

"Oh, just fine, Richard. I'd ask how you slept although I think I already know."

"All right. Listen, I—"

Richard was interrupted by Sylvia as she said, "Look, I noticed something. Brian was shot in his penis. That leads me to believe that Ronald was telling the truth about not killing Brian. I think it was someone to whom Brian was sexually appealing."

Richard looked at her with a stern look. That is exactly what he was about to tell her. He exhaled and decided not to try and take credit for noticing the same thing, as he could never win a debate or argument with Sylvia.

Sarcastically, he said to her, "Now how did we miss that? That is a great angle to explore. How did you possibly think of it?"

Sylvia, not noticing that Richard was being sarcastic, very boldly and bluntly responded.

"Oh, it was when I noticed your erection."

Richard looked down at his erect penis, showing through his boxers. "You were checking me out?"

Sylvia, now in an awkward situation because of her remark, did not respond to his question. Instead, she said, "I'll be going to pick up Ronald in an hour. You want to come?"

"Of course. I'm your partner."

"Firstly, then you will need to go and get dressed. Secondly, you are not my partner. You are just shadowing me."

"Well, doesn't that mean I'm like your temporary partner?"

"Fifty-nine minutes."

Now that he realised that she was keeping track of time, he headed to the elevator and went to his car. As he reached the exit of the police station, the red traffic light stopped him and then a pair of women noticed him. They screamed and yelled out,

"There's Richard 'Castle' King, still in his night gear."

It seemed that every woman for miles around heard and began running towards his car. In a panic, he locked his doors and by the stroke of his luck the traffic light turned green and he burnt rubber just as the crowd of women reached his car.

Back at his penthouse, the problem persisted. Journalists and female fans chased him up to the entrance of the penthouse. He got in and had trouble closing the door because of all the arms and legs trying to get in. He finally managed to close it and he sat by the door and exhaled heavily.

"Man, being famous isn't easy," he said to himself aloud.

That was one heck of a morning. He went to the bathroom and freshened up, got dressed and headed back. Before he left, he was confronted by his daughter who said, "I don't know how you do it, Dad."

"What are you talking about, sweetie?"

"She turned her laptop to him where he saw photos of himself in his boxers and night vest on Twitter."

Embarrassed he exhaled and said sarcastically, "Just my nature."

He headed to the door and was met by the people who had chased him back to the penthouse. He looked back to his daughter with embarrassment and she said, "Go get 'em, Dad."

Richard ran through the crowd and down to his car. He then had to drive around in circles to try and shake his pursuers.

At the station, Sylvia saw that an hour had passed and went to a police van with two officers to pick up Ronald for further questioning. As they set off, Richard pulled up and started to head to the elevator. He then noticed the van leaving and saw Sylvia's reflection from the rear-view mirror.

"Hey! Hey wait up for me! Wait!" he called out to her, as he ran after the van, but she could not hear him. He ran through the underground parking lot after the van and managed to jump onto the back running board and hold onto the handles for the back doors.

As the van drove through the city, the mob of fans and journalists caught sight of him on the back of the van and gave chase. Sylvia eventually noticed the mob chasing the police van and then Richard, desperate to get into the van managed to move along the side of the van and to the driver' door. He smiled and patted away at her window.

Sylvia enjoyed his misery for a second and decided to end it abruptly. She slammed on the brakes and Richard was launched off the side but he managed to grab hold of the rear-view mirror and that changed the direction that he was flying in and he ultimately crashed into the windshield. He quickly got down, jumped in and screamed to Sylvia, "Go! Go! Go!" Sylvia grinned and put her foot down on the accelerator, turned on the siren and sped away.

What a morning that was, for poor Richard.

They finally lost the mob and reached Ronald's place where they took him in for further questioning.

Back at the station they confronted Ronald. "Is this your gun?"

Ronald looked at the gun in the bag in front of him, shocked and confused.

"Ye… Yes. Yah this is my gun but how…? Where did you get it?"

"Where you had someone dispose of it."

"What are you talking about? This is supposed to be locked up in my safe."

"We have it on some authority that this is the gun used to kill

Brian."

"But… I told you I didn't do it!"

"And we believe you. But we cannot if you cannot explain the gun."

"It's supposed to be in the safe back at my place."

"Then why was it buried in a field on the outskirts of New York City?"

"I don't know."

"Where was the gun on the night Brian was killed."

"It was wi…"

There was a long pause and Ronald then got up from the interrogation chair and said in a loud voice, "Oooohhhh THAT BASTARD!"

"What is wrong, Mr Phillips?"

"It is all starting to make sense to me now."

"What is?"

"My gun. I had lent it to someone for that night."

"Who?"

There was a pause and Sylvia and Richard were held in suspense as Ronald began to utter a name to them.

"Ross Lappin."

The look on Richard and Sylvia's faces was priceless. "Why did you lend your gun to a child?"

"Because they had borrowed it from me for ages. They sometimes have these fun nights where they get drunk, high etcetera."

"Then why would they need the gun?"

"Because they liked to 'shoot' at each other with the gun when it was empty. They once told me. They said they loved the adrenaline."

"So why was the gun loaded that night?"

"It was not. Not when I gave it to Ross, at least. I never loaded it. Not once."

"Then why did you have the gun?"

"It was just for show. Remember I was the kingpin of a drug cartel as I told you guys? Well, I needed to look the part. The gun was just for my image. To give me a more gangster-like appearance. It got people to fear and respect me. That's all."

Richard and Sylvia looked at each other. They believed him. However, he was still the one in trouble, unless they found more evidence.

Later, at the desk that they 'shared' they were thinking hard when Richard said to Sylvia, "His story makes sense."

"But the evidence contradicts him."

"However, it does explain why Ross was so nervous around us yesterday."

"Yeah. It does. But we ne—"

Sylvia's phone rang and interrupted what she was saying to Richard. It was the forensic analysist. He confirmed that the ballistics of Ronald's gun were identical to that of the fatal bullet that killed Brian.

Mr Johnson was very pleased when he heard this news. They now had plenty of evidence and confessions from Ronald to send him to prison for at least twenty-five years. But in their guts, Sylvia and Richard both got the feeling that Ronald was being framed.

"Can we hold off on officially charging him for this?"

"Why? We have plenty to put him away for a long time. And you, Detective, will get a huge amount of praise for this. Solving a murder like this in just three days."

"We do not believe he is the killer."

"So? Everyone will buy this story, and they'll love a story of a drug dealer going down for this."

"Yes, we know, and we have enough evidence but he still maintains his innocence. Even with all the confessions he has made."

Richard then jumped into their conversation with, what was most probably the important thing to say in their conversation.

"And I would love to see the drug dealer go down for this too. Now I know I'm new here but aren't we supposed to get the *right* guy for this. Not just the one everyone will believe did it."

Mr Johnson then paused and considered Richard's point about the morality of their job. He nodded lightly and said, "Forty-eight hours." Richard and Sylvia grinned and left. They now had forty-eight hours to find evidence to exonerate Ronald and find the right killer. Their first destination… Mr and Mrs Lappin's house.

Upon their arrival, they were very unwelcome in their house. Mr Lappin claimed that they had really upset their son and for that they were not welcome there. Though, Ross came into the living room and asked his father to please let them in.

"Thank you, Ross," Sylvia said.

"I'm ready to talk now."

"All right."

"He was not supposed to die that night."

Everyone was stunned by his statement, most of all his parents. Sylvia comforted him by saying, "I know. But I need you to tell me what happened that night."

"All right," Ross replied.

He then began to explain to Richard and Sylvia what happened that night. He confirmed that he had borrowed the gun from Ronald, but was unaware that it was loaded. He then went to central park to meet up with his friends.

"We had done it before. Pretending to shoot at each other, because of the adrenaline, and my boyfriend, Brian, particularly enjoyed it when I pretended to shoot at his penis, that's what we did as role-play before sex."

At that moment everyone in the room went silent, as Ross paused and looked over to his parents who were disgusted at what they had just heard.

"B-Brian was gay?" Sylvia asked.

"Yes."

Ross's mother then interrupted and said, "And you are gay too, my son?"

Ross only nodded.

"And you have been sexually active?" Ross nodded again.

"With other boys?"

Again, Ross, too ashamed to speak to his parents, only nodded.

His father gave him a look filled with disgust and left the living room and drove off in his car. His mother stayed behind to hear the rest of the story.

"What happened then?" Richard asked in a compassionate tone.

"Brian always went first whenever we did this, and he wanted me to be the one to 'shoot' him that night. So, I drew the gun... I aimed at his crotch... and then... I pulled the trigger."

Ross broke down and began crying. And in his state said, "But then, I heard one thing I had never heard before. A very loud bang. I looked over to him and he was bleeding profusely from his groin. Seconds later... he was dead."

Ross's mother sat beside him and comforted him. Sylvia and Richard looked at each other and then back at Ross, who then continued with the story.

"I then ran from the park, the others said that they would deal with it. So, I went back to Ronald's house to give him back his gun, but I didn't tell him what happened. Then I came home and waited for the others to tell me what they had done with Brian's body."

"Are you going to charge my son for this?"

"No. I do not think so. It seems clear that someone had this planned. We cannot charge Ross for this."

"Thank you."

Sylvia looked at Mrs Lappin and then to Ross, who was crying in her arms.

"You are a very brave young man. Thank you for telling us the truth. Now, I promise, we will find the one responsible for this."

Richard and Sylvia left. They were both processing their emotions until they reached the station again.

"You know what the weird thing is, Richard?"

"The fact that our anonymous source's information is supported by all the evidence we have even though we do not believe their story?"

"What?"

"Isn't that what you were about to say?"

Sylvia thought about it and Richard had a point, and although it was not really what she was thinking, she responded, "Oh, yes of course."

Whoever was behind that distorted voice knew far too much and was their missing link. They both agreed that they needed to find out who it was. But their luck was out. Whenever they tried to call that number, they couldn't get through, from any phone. And they couldn't trace the number or its signal either. All they had was the conversations which were not recorded and the photo of the plans that they had sent, which were supposedly Ronald's.

Soon, night had fallen, and while racking her brain, Sylvia got very tired. They did not have very much time left and they needed something. Sylvia eventually decided to go home. Richard told her that he would stay a little while longer.

"All right. Just don't fall asleep in my chair in your night gear again."

Richard smiled, feeling insulted and watched her walk away.

As he went through the file again, he looked very closely at the photo of the plan that had been sent to them. He stared at it for almost two hours and he decided to give up for the day. He took his suit jacket from the back of Sylvia's chair and took a step away when he noticed something he had missed in the photo.

In the top corner of the image was, what looked to be a pendant. A necklace with an imitation of the Eiffel tower hanging from it. Richard examined it. He knew he had seen it before. But where?

He then went home to think about who he had seen wearing that necklace recently. He had a fine eye for jewellery because of his mother and sister, who had very expensive taste and an eye for detail. It had been an extremely long day for him, given what had happened that morning and so he just went to his bed and instantly fell asleep. When he woke up the next morning, he had a shower and got dressed and prepared breakfast for his mother and daughter, since he did not join them for dinner the previous night.

He stuck a note on the refrigerator that said, '*Enjoy! It's both your favourites,*' and left headed to the police station. As he got into his car, it hit him, the necklace... it was the one Nicole wore. Before he got out of the parking area, he went onto Facebook and searched for Nicole Bandeira. There, in almost every picture she had uploaded on Facebook, was that silver necklace with the Eiffel tower hanging around her neck. He smiled, put his phone on the car's wireless charging pad and drove off to the station.

He arrived to find Sylvia already at her desk, racking her brain again.

"I found out who our informant is," he announced to her.

"How?"

Richard took the photo of the plans and pointed out the necklace on the desk, in the top corner. Sylvia examined it and looked up to Richard's face.

"I've seen this before."

"I know."

"Who is it?"

Richard took out his phone and put the Facebook picture of Nicole in front of Sylvia. The two smiled and made their way to Mr and Mrs Bandeira's house.

They questioned Nicole as to whether or not she was their anonymous source. When they searched her room, they found a locked box under her bed, with a phone inside. They turned it on and called Sylvia's phone with it. When they listened, it scrambled their voices. They knew they had the right phone.

They went back to the living room and confronted Nicole with what they found, and asked her to come with them to the station.

"Is she under arrest?" her parents asked.

"No, ma'am."

As they walked towards the door, Richard had a flush of thoughts go through his mind. He turned to Nicole and said, "It was you, wasn't it?"

Nicole looked up at Richard, grinned deviously and then ran, out the door and into the street. She fled and eluded them. Though she could not go very far. Two hours later, she was picked up by police officers at the edge of town. She was arrested and brought to the station, where Richard and Sylvia were waiting.

"What makes you think she did it?" Sylvia asked Richard as they waited for Nicole to arrive.

"You'll see soon enough."

The doors of the station opened and officers escorted Nicole to the interrogation room.

"Shall we?"

"Let's."

Richard and Sylvia entered the interrogation room, while two officers and Nicole's parents stood outside watching.

Sylvia began the interrogation. "Why did you run?"

Nicole looked over to Richard and smiled, but kept quiet.

"Nicole, if you do not talk, the charges and the punishment will be much harsher."

"Your novelist-partner already knows everything. I can see that in his eyes."

"You see if he tells me, you could serve over ten years. Talk, and maybe you'll only serve about five."

Nicole considered, and agreed to tell them the story.

"I fell in love with Brian. He had been my friend for a long time, but I fell in love with him, all right? That's when I decided to leave Ronald. Brian just had something that Ronald did not, and whatever it was, it was something I wanted in a man. However shortly after I ended my relationship with Ronald, I learnt that Brian was…"

Richard took over when Nicole paused. "Gay?"

"Yes. That he was already involved with Ross. I was broken hearted. The thought that the guy I was in love with would rather put his penis into another guy's anus rather than my vagina…

that he did not want my breasts in his face… that he wouldn't want me to be his wife… those thoughts drove me over the edge."

"And that's when you developed your plan for revenge against him."

"Correct. I broke into Ronald's place with the spare key he had made for me, when we were still dating. I had seen the code for his safe whenever he had taken the gun out for us to play with when we had sex. I took the gun, and put one round in the chamber and put it back in the safe and the rest was filled in for me."

"You knew that Brian always got 'shot' at first, so no matter who pulled the trigger, the bullet would hit him."

"Exactly. So, I stood around and watched at Ross pulled the trigger on Brian and watch him bleed to death from his crotch. Then I sent Ross to give the gun back to Ronald, and the rest of us stayed behind to move his body."

"That's when you took one of Brian's testicles. Why?"

"You know how a girl's eggs can be fertilised via a surrogate? I was planning something similar. To extract the sperm and semen from his testicle and impregnate myself. I wanted to carry his child. But the thought of having to raise a child alone, without a father, did not work for me. So, I disposed of it in the fish pond. I was just going to pin it all on Ronald, and make sure that things moved quickly by feeding the police the info I wanted them to know."

The story horrified everyone. That such evil could brew out of the love that someone had for someone else. Nicole's parents, outside the interrogation room, stared in horror at the monster they had birthed into the world.

Sylvia and Richard left her in the room and went to Mr Johnson's office to report that they had solved the case. With about twenty-four hours still on the clock.

They charged Nicole for the murder of Brian and let Ronald go. He would still have to serve time for his other crimes that he admitted to, but he would not be charged for Brian's murder.

Nicole was charged and did not get bail, she would await her trial which would take place in three months, in prison.

That evening, Richard and Sylvia sat at their desk and breathed a sigh of relief. They had caught the killer, and were very proud of themselves. Mr Johnson came over to them and said to Sylvia, "So, wasn't Richard here a good partner?"

As much as she did not want to say 'yes', she had to admit she probably could not have caught Nicole without him.

Feeling proud of himself, and with his ego burning, he asked Sylvia to join him and his family for dinner.

Sylvia declined his offer, which did hurt Richard's ego.

They went home separately. Richard got home with plenty of time to spare and he decided to prepare dinner for his daughter and mother. They ate dinner together and Richard played with his daughter for a bit. After they went to bed, Richard went to his laptop and started typing away the next chapter of his book that he was basing on the case they had just solved.

When he eventually checked the time, it was three o'clock in the morning, and he decided to go to bed. As he lay in bed, the only thing on his mind was Sylvia, and Sylvia, in her bed was thinking of Richard.

Richard then went to bed knowing that Sylvia would call when they had another homicide case to work.

Chapter 6

A week and a half later, Sylvia was sitting at her desk. She had to admit to herself that she did miss having Richard around, a bit. His humorous and yet ingenious nature was quite a nice thing to have around, however she was still trying to come up with a way to get rid of him. She was still afraid that he would fall in love with her, as she was oblivious to the fact that he was already in love with her, from eight and a half years ago. Her other great fear was that she might end up falling in love with him.

Her phone rang, while she was lost in thought. It was her colleague. There had been a murder, and she was needed on the scene. She exhaled, put on her jacket and called Richard as she headed to the elevator.

Richard was playing video games in virtual reality, with Nathalie, his daughter, when his phone rang. It was Sylvia. He knew it meant that there was another case for them to work. He was hoping that their next case would come up soon, as he needed to spend as much time with her as possible so he could make his move on her, and his wish had now come true. A bit sooner than he had expected it to, as well.

He answered the call with a very extraordinary remark.

"Who was murdered and was it brutal?"

"Level thirty-three, south tower. Now!"

A very brief call that was. Richard had to cut fun time with his daughter a bit short, he headed to the door, put on his coat, like a child, he informed his mother that he was going out, and left. When he got to his car, he put the address into the GPS, and he discovered that, shockingly, the crime scene was just four blocks away. It sent a cold chill down his spine. A murder committed so close to his home.

He arrived on scene before Sylvia. He then foolishly tried to enter the crime scene where crime scene investigators were working.

"Make way, Detective King on scene."

An officer blocked his path and pointed out that he was not a detective and that he could not enter without Sylvia, the real detective, present. He waited for what seemed like three hours, even though it was only about five minutes, and Sylvia arrived.

"How'd you get here before me?"

"I practically live around the corner."

Sylvia looked at him, scoffed and they then entered the crime scene. It was a very luxurious apartment.

"Small," Richard said. But upon opening his mouth to speak he could smell and almost taste a horrible stench.

"What do we got?" Sylvia asked Sophia and her team of investigators. Her question had a very obvious answer. Right in front of her, was the corpse of a woman, in a very odd place.

"Victim identified as a Ms Julia Payton."

"What did they do to her?" Richard asked as he scanned the gruesome scene.

"Stabbed to death. Three lacerations on neck, two on her left breast, six to her torso, and most notably, one to her cervix."

"And...?" Richard continued as he stared at where the victim had been placed.

"Based on the degree of rigor mortis, not long after she was killed, the perpetrator then moved her body from the living room, where she died, and stuffed her corpse in the safe."

"Well, the murder was brutal. Satisfied, Richard?" Sylvia said, as a reference to the question he had asked when he answered her call.

"Does it look like we have a motive?"

"Yep. Robbery. All her jewellery was taken, along with her wedding ring and finger."

Sylvia walked around, looking to see if she could find anything else. Richard stood around and saw something that caught his attention. The shelf on the right side of the room was slightly out of place.

"Well, this was definitely not a random robbery," Richard said.

"How can you tell?"

Richard pushed a book that was on the shelf and it fell through. There was no wall behind the shelf. Richard and Sylvia pushed the shelf out of the way and discovered a secret room, with display cabinets. They were all empty, but it was clear that they had housed jewellery.

"If it was someone random, they wouldn't have known about this secret room. It's pretty well hidden."

Sylvia grinned to herself. Just like the last two cases she and Richard had worked together; he was already proving to have his uses. Sophia then said to them, "It might also explain the stab to her cervix, but upon first inspection, it looks like she got away from her attacker at some point and then stabbed in the vagina as a last resort to stop her moving."

Sylvia and Richard looked around. They would have another tough case on their hands. And a very deadly killer to catch.

Back at the station, they sat and waited for a personal profile of Julia to be presented to them. An officer then came to them and read the first page of the profile to them.

"Julia Payton. Recently divorced. No children. Occupation, owner of a range of five-star restaurants called 'Karamello'."

"Who did she divorce?"

"One Codey Payton. A computer programmer."

"Why did they divorce?"

"Apparently, Codey cheated on her and Julia couldn't take it."

Richard and Sylvia now had the perfect first suspect. Someone who knew Julia, would have known about the secret room in her apartment, had motive to kill her and it would have all explained why her wedding finger was taken after she was killed and why the killing was so brutal. But if there was something they had learnt from their previous case, just because you have the perfect suspect, doesn't make them guilty.

Nevertheless, they had to go and visit Codey. Upon their arrival, Codey was shocked to hear that his ex-wife was dead.

Sylvia was very uncompassionating towards Codey, and went ahead with the standard questions that she had to ask Codey.

"Where were you last night?"

"I was at the airport, picking up my cousin."

"You have anyone who can verify this?"

"Yes. My cousin, who is asleep in the next room."

"Why is he still asleep at this hour in the afternoon?"

"His flight was delayed yesterday. We only arrived here around four o'clock this morning."

He tried to hold his own, but began to shed a few tears. Both Richard and Sylvia looked at each other and then Richard said something out of the ordinary to him.

"You still loved her, didn't you?"

"Yes," Codey replied, still trying to hold his tears in.

"They why did you divorce her?"

"My mother. She forced me to. She said that if I didn't, she'd cut me out of her will and leave her whole estate to my brother, Merritt."

"Why did she want you to divorce Julia?"

"She... she wanted grand children from me, and so when she found out that Julia couldn't have children, she just wanted her out of the family."

"What do you mean she 'couldn't'?"

Codey began to let his tears flow and said, "We had tried to have kids, three times, but Julia... she had miscarriages all three times and that's when she was told by her gynaecologist that..."

There was a very long pause as Codey began to cry heavily.

"That what?"

"She had a weak cervix."

Codey fell off the sofa and cried as hard as he could on the floor. He cried so loudly that the entire house seemed to shake. Sylvia and Richard agreed to leave Codey to grieve in peace, and they headed back to the station. On the way, Richard pointed out that it could very well be Codey's mother who murdered Julia. It would perfectly explain the stab wound that they were narrowing the investigation on.

Back at the station, they got the profile of Abigail Payton, Codey's mother. The idea of her being the killer was eliminated by the fact that she was seventy-two years old, and unable to even walk, as she was in a wheel chair. She could not have been the killer.

Also, with CCTV evidence supplied to them from the airport, they were able to eliminate Codey as a suspect, as they saw him, sitting around in the lobby, waiting for his cousin and he then left around three-thirty in the morning. Since it seemed that Julia was killed around one o'clock that morning, they eliminated him as a suspect.

With no other leads, evidence or anything of the sort, the investigation was off to a slow start, which was very bad for them.

Sylvia got stressed and went to the department's shooting range. She shot at the paper image of a person and Richard then walked in.

Hearing the gunshots so close to him did rattle his nerves a bit, or at least that's what he wanted Sylvia to believe, that it was his first time hearing gunshots. Sylvia continued to fire and eventually Richard shouted out to her, "Wouldn't it be more challenging if the target was moving?"

Sylvia stopped and considered his point. It was a good point. Richard then continued and said, "You should also reposition your stance, it's making your aim weak."

Sylvia looked at him and smiled, then arrogantly said, "Okay, why don't you show me how it's done then?"

Richard's eyes lit up like a child who had been given a thousand dollars. He took some safety goggles and ear muffs from the shelf behind them and Sylvia handed him the gun.

He aimed, posing as if he was in a blockbuster movie. Sylvia looked at him, giggled and said, "You're not in a movie, here. Left leg bent, right straight. Left hand under the gun. There, now... now shoot."

Richard pulled the trigger in the pose that Sylvia had put him in. After the shot, the paper was intact. The bullet did not even make it to the paper. Embarrassed, he pulled again. This time the shot hit the paper, but not the image of the person at all.

"You'll get better," Sylvia said as she giggled.

"All right. Hey, I came to ask; I see the other officers managed to get photos of some of the jewellery that was stolen from Julia."

"Yeah? And?"

"I was wondering if I could take them home to examine them."

Sylvia looked at him and scoffed. "What? You think you can find something I can't?"

"I think I've done so before. Very recently actually."

He pulled the trigger again. This time the bullet went through the image's groin. Richard and Sylvia both cried out, "Ooouuuhhhh, that's going to hurt."

Sylvia was now considering the point Richard had just made. He was right, he had found vital evidence in their past two cases that she had missed. Because of that she could not entirely deny him, but the rules stated that she could not just let him take police files home.

Then she had an idea. She grinned at given what a bad shot he had proven to be, she said to him, "Tell you what. You get any of the next three shots into the ten zone, I'll let you take the file home."

"Really?"

"Really."

"You promise?"

"Promise," Sylvia commented arrogantly, as she was so confident that he could not do it.

Richard aimed and fired three times, rapidly. All three went right through the ten zone of the target. Sylvia removed her ear muffs and goggles simultaneously, and checked to see if her eyes were deceiving her. But they weren't.

"You are a very good teacher. I'll see you in the morning."

Richard went to their desk and took the file and headed home, leaving Sylvia in the shooting range, with her eyes widened and her jaw on the floor. She wanted to stop Richard from taking the file, but she was a woman of her word, and she had to make good on her promise. She only hoped that no one would find out.

Back at his penthouse, his mother prepared dinner and his daughter did her homework in her room while Richard sat in the living room examining the evidence photos of Julia's jewellery that had been stolen. When Nathalie was done, she sat with her father and hugged him.

"What are you doing?"

"Analysing evidence."

"These look really nice," she commented, as she looked at the photo of a necklace encrusted with at least thirty sapphires. His mother then came and stood behind the sofa that they were sitting on, with a glass of wine and said, "Dinner will be ready in… Oh ho hooooo, well well well, where have you been all my life", as she took the photo that Richard was holding, from his hand. Richard did not even bother trying to take it back from her, as he knew how much she loved jewels.

"Now THIS. Ohhhh, this is something Mark would have got for me. Unlike my dearest son."

Richard only heard up to the name 'Mark'. Now, he was frozen in his thoughts, but was woken by his daughter.

"Who's Mark?"

Yvonne then said to Richard, "Why did you have to end us, Richard?"

Richard still did not respond, and Nathalie, very confused, asked again, "Who is Mark?"

Richard seemed to have forgotten how to talk, and his mother just continued, "It was not just us you ended; it was his whole career."

Nathalie could not take the suspense and curiosity any more. She asked again, in a louder voice, "Who is Mark?"

Richard then seemed to regain his ability to talk and finally answered her question.

"Do you remember that character in my third book?"

"The gem lover turned criminal dude?"

"Yeah, I kind of based him off Mark."

"What?"

Yvonne then added, "Yes, darling, and he was also once my fiancé."

Nathalie was shocked and confused by what had just befallen her ears. Her grandmother then began to explain that Richard had snitched on Mark for an inaccurate evaluation he had made on a museum exhibit of jewels. He was then fired and turned into a notorious jewel thief, except unlike in Richard's book, he had never been caught.

"I think I'm going to visit him."

"Do you even know where to find him?"

"Yes, I think so."

"He'll kill you, I'm sure he hasn't forgotten what you did to him."

"Maybe he's forgiven me," Richard said, though he highly doubted it.

"All right. If you find him and survive the encounter, tell him he owes me a diamond encrusted photo frame, for the one he stole."

"Will do, Mother. Don't dish up for me."

And with that, Richard left the penthouse and drove off into the night, to an abandoned flat. Beside the flat itself, was a door, that he knew lead to an underground room that Mark had once shown him, before Richard betrayed him. If he was right, Mark would still be there, because there was something there that Mark would not have abandoned.

He entered the room. There he found things. Magnifying glasses, emeralds, rubies, sapphires, but what really stood out to him were some photos. They were identical to those in the case file he had been looking at.

Then… POW! Richard was struck with a punch, as he turned around when he heard some footsteps behind him. He was knocked to the ground, and looked up and saw his attacker. Mark!

"Hello… Castle."

Richard sat on the floor with his hands up, to protect himself, but to his surprise, Mark did not continue his attack. Instead, he giggled at Richard, as he cowardly sat before him on the floor, he then turned around and said, "Get up, old friend."

"That's it? You aren't going to kill me?"

"Last I checked, I'm a thief, not a murderer. You want a drink?"

"Uhmm, yes please, old friend."

"On the rocks?"

"Yep. Oh, by the way, my mother sends her regards. She says you owe her a diamond encrusted photo frame."

Mark giggled and the two had a fun few minutes of catching up, when Mark addressed the elephant in the room.

"So, what did you want from me?"

"I need your help."

"Engagement ring shopping, are we?"

"No. I'm working a police investigation."

Mark froze and stared up at Richard in wonder. "I did not realise you were a cop."

"I'm not. I'm shadowing a detective for my next book."

"All right, what do you need?"

"I need information on some jewels. The ones in those photos you have over there."

Mark looked at the photos. He was curious. He admitted was planning to steal them himself, until he discovered some even more regal ones. When Richard informed him that someone had killed Julia for them, Mark said he thought he could help, but he needed something to do so. He needed to see the crime scene.

"I can't let you into the crime scene."

"Thought you were the detective's temp partner."

"Even I can't go in there without her."

"Then good luck to you."

Mark turned and began to walk away. Richard then thought to himself, and remembered what this was all about, impressing and winning Sylvia over. He then called out to Mark, and reluctantly agreed to take him to the crime scene.

They arrived and found the door locked. Mark picked it and they went in. Richard then locked the door from inside, where he found the key on a nightstand. They walked through the room with two small torches, and Mark looked around curiously.

"Come on, Mark, we can't stay here for long."

Mark then turned to face Richard and noticed the safe behind him. He noticed that there were blood stains around it, which had come from inside.

"You did not mention that they stuffed her in a safe."

"Is that significant in any way?"

"Richard, there are only two types of jewel thieves. There's my kind. We do it for the love of jewels and valuables. We do not hurt people. We are ghosts. Get in, take and get out, before anyone even knows you are there."

"And the second kind?"

"The second kind, those are the ones who steal for their survival. They do not mind killing, IF they need to kill. Usually, they are poor and uneducated. But this…"

He paused and held Richard in suspense.

"But this what?"

"But whoever did this. They were not doing it for the jewels. If they took the time to kill her first and stuff her in the safe before taking anything… this was something personal."

Mark had just confirmed what Richard had initially thought. Her killer was someone close to her.

"So, the jewels?"

"Oh, they appear very valuable. Authentic. Pretty sure someone could clear half a million dollars easily, by selling it all."

Then, the unexpected happened. The door handle began to shake. Someone was trying to get in. Richard began to panic and turned to the door, trying to see some way to escape. When he turned around to talk to Mark, he was gone, and Richard was now standing all alone in the room, with no clue what to do.

He looked to the door again and began to sweat in fear slightly. He turned around again and tried to find a place to hide. But it was too late. The door opened and Richard, with his back to the door put his hands up and turned around assuming that the killer was returning to the scene. When he completed the turn, he was both shocked and relieved to see Sylvia at the door, aiming her gun at him.

"Richard?"

"Well, hello, Detective."

Sylvia exhaled heavily and asked him what he was doing there. Richard answered with a question of his own, "What are you doing here, Sylvia?"

"Checking to see if there was something I missed."

They stood in the apartment a while and then decided to go home. Richard got home to find his mother and daughter sleeping peacefully, and did not disturb them.

The next morning, at the station, Richard told Sylvia that he had brought Mark to the crime scene and he had given him some important information. Sylvia gave him and earful about bringing an unauthorised person to the scene, but she forgave him, as the information it had brought to their attention would be useful.

Then, every investigator's worst nightmare came true for them. Sylvia's phone rang. When she hung up, she looked at Richard in shock and said, "There's been another murder."

Richard and Sylvia arrived on scene, to find a woman's body hanging from a bedsheet, tied to a fancy light in her apartment. They were just seven blocks away from where the first murder took place. Sophia gave them a basic breakdown. The case had very much the same MO. Woman stabbed to death, multiple lacerations. A lot of valuable jewellery stolen. The main two differences were, the woman was not stabbed in her cervix, and she was not stuffed in a safe.

"Although, we do have the killer's signature now."

"What do you mean?"

"She's got two stab wounds on her left breast."

It made it clear to Richard and Sylvia that they now had a serial killer on their hands.

The woman was later identified as Henley Allan. A very successful actress. Unmarried and had no children. There did not seem to be any connection between the two victims. One was in the entertainment industry, the other in the food business. The only apparent common thing be that they were rich and had a lot of jewellery.

The killer seemed to be getting smarter. He did not leave very much behind. No DNA, no prints, nothing, and that would make him hard to catch. The only thing was that he did not hide his motive behind the killings, as he always did something out of the ordinary with the corpse. First victim was stuffed in a safe, the other hung from her light.

It all coincided with what Mark said, whoever was behind it was doing it to take the lives of the jewel owners, not their jewellery.

With no new evidence or suspects, Richard and Sylvia were stuck at a standstill, until three days later when a third victim was found. Molly Grimshaw. She was stabbed to death, had two stabs to her left breasts, and her corpse spread out on her kitchen stove. She also had a lot of jewellery and it was all missing.

The killer was getting better, and they were falling behind. Her profile showed that she was divorced and that she was very successful in the law industry as an attorney. But there was one difference between her and the previous two victims. She had a child. From one of her earliest relationships. Which meant that they had the sad task of informing Molly's twenty-two-year-old daughter about her mother's sad fate.

As they drove to where Molly's daughter lived, Richard and Sylvia both felt defeated. These two murders could have been prevented if they had done more. But what more could they do?

There was still something very odd about the information that they had. The three had no apparent connection. They were all rich and had plenty of jewellery, but they worked in different industries and did not have any apparent connection. So, the biggest question they were trying to answer was,

How did the killer know all three of them?

Chapter 7

They arrived at the home of Yolanda Grimshaw, Molly's daughter, and she was shattered by the news of her mother's passing, like any person would be. Sylvia asked her if she had ever heard of the names Julia Payton or Henley Allan.

"No. Who are they? Did they do this?"

"No. They... they were the two victims before your mother." Yolanda was now even more shocked and appalled.

"There were others?"

"Yes."

"Then why hasn't the killer been caught yet? You are supposed to keep people safe! If you two were doing your job and caught this guy, then my mother would still be alive!"

Sylvia, being a detective, was used to being blamed for people dying when there was a serial killer on the loose, so she did not take Yolanda's words personally.

"I know how it feels to lose a parent, Yolanda. And for the next few days, you are going to play out every possible way that you could have saved your mother. *'If only I had gone to visit her that night.' 'If only the police had been doing their job.'* But believe me it won't change anything. But you can still avenge your mother by helping us."

"Helping you how?"

"We need to find what the connection between these three women are. And fast... before the killer strikes again. Because so far, we have not found any connection between the three of them."

Richard then pointed out the one thing that they did know, and if he hadn't, the case may never have been solved.

"Except of the fact that they all owned a large amount of valuable jewellery."

Yolanda looked over to her right, at Richard, and widened her eyes at him.

"How do you know my mother owned a lot of jewellery?"

"It was all stolen."

Yolanda paused and looked back to Sylvia, on her left, and then back at Richard.

"Very few people know that my mother owned jewellery."

"What do you mean?"

Yolanda paused and looked over to the fireplace, at a family photo. She walked over to it, picked it up and went back to the couch, and handed Sylvia the photo. Sylvia looked down at the photo and then back up at Yolanda, with a puzzled expression. She did not understand what Yolanda was trying to show her. Yolanda realised this and began to explain.

"My mother never wore her jewellery, except to special events. That photo was on my grandmother's one hundredth birthday. It's the only photo I have of her with her jewellery on."

That was a very valuable clue, but they needed to narrow it down a bit. Richard then asked her, "What kind of special events?"

"Fund raisers, charities, big birthdays, award ceremonies. Things like that."

Richard then began to think to himself. He thought he had an idea. Sylvia began to ask her some more standard questions, like who had a grudge with her mother and who knew her habits the best. With very unsatisfactory answers from her, Sylvia and

Richard decided to leave.

As they drove off to the police station, Richard said to Sylvia, "Well, at least now we have a clue to work with."

"What are you talking about?"

"What did we say all our victims had in common?"

"They all had a substantial amount of jewellery?"

"And?"

Sylvia paused and thought for a while, but she could not figure it out, so Richard did for her.

"They were all rich."

"So? What's your point? We already know that they worked in different industries."

"If they were all rich, what do you think they would all do?"

Sylvia paused again. She was growing tiresome of Richard's Riddles.

"Quit talking in tongues, Castle. Out with it. What are you thinking?"

"They probably all did charity work. I mean it is the best way to let everyone else know that you are rich. That's why I do it. Mostly."

"You think they did some kind of charity work together?"

"Exactly. And if they did…"

"That would have been how the killer knew them all."

"Exactly."

Sylvia was intrigued by Richard's angle, and since they had no other lead to follow, she called ahead to the station and had them pull the attendance lists of all the fund raisers and charity event that had taken place in New York over the course of the last three months.

When they got back to the station, they began to write down all the events that Molly, Henley and Julia had attended. They could not see any events that they had all attended, and were about to call it a dead end, until Richard noticed something.

"Wait, wait, wait, look!"

"What?"

"Molly went to a fund raiser hosted by Happy Helpers."

Another investigator then noticed something and said with enthusiasm, "Henley went to a fund raiser held by Happy Helpers to the Disabled and Less Fortunate."

Richard then said, "What an unimaginative name."

Sylvia then looked at the events Julia attended and noticed the last thing they needed.

"Julia, went to an event held by HHDLF."

"It's the same place."

"So, that is most likely where the killer met all three of them."

Richard then went onto his phone and looked up the organisation. As their luck would have it, it seemed that the fund raiser was so successful on the night that the three victims had attended, that they were having another fund raiser that very night. The four all looked at each other and Sylvia and the other two investigators stared at Richard. He may have just saved another person from being killed, because if they had got this clue a few hours later, there may have very well been another death.

"We have to go in there."

"Yes, but not like this."

"What do you mean?"

"If we go in like this, we're going to scare the guy away. We'll stand out too much."

Sylvia and the two investigators, who were now helping with the investigation looked down at what they were wearing. Richard had a point. Richard then looked at Sylvia and said,

"Let's go tonight. As guests."

"You mean as in... as in like a... a date."

To Richard that's exactly what it was supposed to be, but he had to deny it.

"No, it's official business. And you two, you need to be nearby, in case we catch him."

They did not like being given orders. Especially by someone who was not a cop, but they all agreed that he had the best plan possible.

"But, Castle, we—"

"Pick me up at eight?"

"Wha...?"

Sylvia did not get the chance to say anything as Richard was already going home, to get ready. Sylvia was quite frustrated, but she knew this was the best possible plan, and since Richard was so well known, it would help them blend in and hopefully find the killer.

Sylvia left and went home to get ready. She asked Sophia to come with her, as she was not very good at 'dressing up'. When she got out of the shower, she looked through her wardrobe for something to wear. She then put on each of the few dresses she had in front of her and Sophia gave her opinion.

Of the seven dresses she had as options to wear that night, they were either too sexy, too cheap looking or too shiny, and none of those things would cut the mustard that night. Sylvia needed to appear rich and classy, like every other woman who would be there that night. Sylvia was stuck, until they heard her doorbell ring. Since she was still just wrapped in a towel, from her shower, she had Sophia answer it. It was a delivery. A very large white box.

Sylvia was quite confused, and Sophia was very curious as

to what was inside. Sophia put the box down and opened the lid. There was something very large, wrapped in white foil paper, and right on top was a note.

"What does it say?" Sylvia asked, as she walked over to the box and looked at the large object. Sophia sat on the bed and read out to her what was on the note.

'Let down your hair.'

Sylvia thought to herself for a second.

"Let down your…"

It hit her, she figured it all out and looked over to Sophia.

"Rapunzel. It's from HIM."

Sophia understood and it hit her too.

"Oh! It's a dress. Now open it up."

"Open it up? No way! Does he think I'll just… oh!"

Sylvia was agitated at first, because she hated being told how to dress by others, but as she unwrapped the dress in the box, she had to admit, it was a pretty good choice. It was perfect, and to a certain degree, it was her style. It managed to give off the appearance of both sexual attractiveness and class. Plus, she did not have very much other choice of something to wear that night. So, she put on the dress and had Sophia do her hair and make-up, then went to pick up Richard.

At his penthouse, Richard also had a problem to put up with, but it was not to do with his clothes. It was his mother. Whenever she saw him put on his tuxedo and asked Nathalie to put his tie on for him, she knew it meant there was a high-class event, and given how she loved such events, she wanted to go.

"Come on, why won't you tell me where the party is?"

"Because you'll show up," Richard bluntly said to his mother as she followed him around the penthouse, as he got ready.

The doorbell rang while Nathalie was still fixing her father's tie for him and so Richard asked his mother to get it for him. It was Sylvia, as expected, but what they had not expected, was for her to look so good.

It was the very first time Richard had ever seen her wearing make-up and the dress he had bought for her looked just perfect on her. A high class, glossy red dress. But to Yvonne, who had very high classy taste, something was missing.

"You look beautiful, Detective."

"Thank you. I wish I could say the same for you, Castle," she said sarcastically in reply as Yvonne walked back into the living room.

"Here you go, darling," she said as she strung a silver necklace incrusted with rubies around Sylvia's neck.

"Oh, no, Yvonne, I... I couldn't."

"Now come on, you'll need it more than me tonight." She spun Sylvia around to make her face the mirror.

"There. Perfect," Yvonne commented and Sylvia had to agree. She could not remember ever having looked so good in all her life.

"So, where are you two going?"

Richard looked up and gestured to Sylvia not to tell her where they were really going. Sylvia noticed, but, as she like to make him feel miserable, she grinned and said to Yvonne, "We're going to a fund raiser held downtown by the HHDLF."

Richard stared at her with his eyes half shut and his mouth straight. Sylvia always was unbelievable, in a good and bad way, but he hoped that his mother wouldn't show up. Though he had his doubts. When Richard finished dressing, he and Sylvia left and got into Sylvia's car and drove off.

They stopped a block away from where the event was to

meet the other two investigators, who had arranged a limousine to drop them off.

When Sylvia and Richard got in, they stared at Sylvia, or more specifically her boobs. When Sylvia noticed, she reminded them that she could slap hard, so they faced forward and drove Richard and Sylvia to the venue. When they dropped them off, they hid the limousine in a nearby alleyway and went to the entrance, where they posed as security guards.

Now inside the venue, Sylvia was very uncomfortable. She felt like she did not belong in such a crowdie place, with such rich people.

"Would you like a drink?"

"Yes. A double. On the rocks."

Richard knew when Sylvia was being sarcastic, and this was most definitely not one of those times. He had never pegged Sylvia for a whiskey woman, but what could he do? He began to walk off to the bar when Sylvia stopped him, "But, I'm on duty, so... water."

Richard was now much more comfortable. He went and got her and himself a glass of water. As they sipped away at their glasses of water, Richard noticed something. Or someone rather.

"Oh, you little..." he exclaimed and speedily walked after the man. Sylvia followed suit, wondering who he had seen.

It was Mark. He had stopped walking and was whispering to the event organiser.

"How could you do this, Mark?"

"I'm sorry, Richard."

"You played me for a fool."

"It was just supposed to be a joke."

"A joke? Three people are DEAD!"

Mark's smug smile fell from his face. Now he was confused.

"Dead? What are you talking about? Oh, are you talking about the murders? Come on, Rick, I told you, I'm a ghost and a thief. Not a killer."

Sylvia joined them, and had no clue what they had just spoken about. Richard was now very confused. Why was he at the event then?

"Then what were you whispering about?"

Mark grinned, and pointed his finger to the stage. Richard had been totally oblivious to the fact that someone had been giving a speech. As the person who was speaking walked off the stage, his greatest fear had come true. His mother walked onto the stage. There was an auction starting, and the money they got from the bids was going to go to helping the less fortunate and disabled. He then realised that his mother was going to be the auctioneer.

She began the auction, "The first item we have is a signed copy of my son's first book. And there he is, my beautiful son."

As she said this, a bright spotlight came on and shone on Sylvia and Richard. Richard awkwardly put up his hand, at shoulder height and waved around as his mother continued to speak.

"My still single son. Now whoever wins the book will also get to spend a night in my son's company. Okay, can we see five hundred dollars?"

A young woman instantly put her hand up and Richard looked over to her and put on an awkward smile. Sylvia, who was by his side, wore a large smile as she enjoyed Richard being embarrassed in front of the audience.

"All right, we have five hundred from this lovely lady. Can we see one thousand?"

Now, a young gay man put his hand up and Richard's eyes

widened with fear and embarrassment.

"We have a gentleman, with one thousand. Can we see two thousand?"

Richard stopped paying attention to the auction and slowly and very shakily turned his head around to face Mark.

"Now, we're even," Mark said to Richard as he patted his shoulder, turned around and walked away with the event organiser. Richard turned around and looked to his right at Sylvia. He had to do something. He was now desperate. Wearing his desperate smile, he faced Sylvia and said, "Okay, lo… look, you know I have money. Whatever you pay for the book… I'll pay you back. Doub… triple!"

Sylvia smiled even more, the desperation on Richard's face was priceless, and she was not going to make it any easier for him.

"Not a chance in hell, Castle."

The next thing Richard heard was that the book had been sold, and he did not even want to see who had won. About half an hour later, the auction was over and they announced that they had raised one hundred and fifty thousand dollars. It was impressive. Then people began to dance and Sylvia and Richard danced as well. While they were dancing, Sylvia noticed a waiter, who appeared to be taking a selfie with some woman who was all alone.

She looked at the woman's neck and noticed that she had a very fine necklace on. She reckoned that she was onto something. After the dance, she quickly walked outside and ordered the two detectives to come in and help her arrest the waiter.

Richard looked confused when he saw them walk in and went with the to the waiter, who was still with the lonely woman, and seemed to be flirting with her.

"Sir?"

"Yes?"

"Detective Beckette, NYPD, you are under arrest on suspicion of murder," Sylvia said, showing him her badge, like she did when arresting anyone.

Richard was confused and the waiter appeared to be as well. The woman quickly stood up and walked away. The waiter called out to her but it was no use, as he was already being handcuffed and taken away.

"Where was the badge?" Richard asked.

"Don't ask."

The waiter was taken to the station and spent the night there, waiting for Sylvia and Richard to interrogate him, which would only happen the next morning.

When morning came, Sylvia and Richard questioned him, but he claimed that he was innocent, and blamed them for ruining his night, as he was planning to sleep with the woman he was with. Richard understood his pain, but Sylvia was not sympathetic. The guy had clearly been in trouble with the law before, he knew the rules of an interrogation, and he knew he was free to leave as long as he was not charged. With no evidence to charge him on, they had no choice but to let him go.

When they sat at their desk, their assistants brought them his file. The waiter was identified as Blake Fall. He'd only got out of prison a month ago, for raping his ex-girlfriend. Before that, he was actually a very successful events co-ordinator.

Richard and Sylvia both had a gut feeling that they had just let the killer out of the station. But, alas, without proof, they couldn't do anything.

That's when something crossed Richard's mind. If he was only recently released from prison, he would need money. That might explain why he would steal the jewellery, after the murders.

"I think I have something. Come with me, Detective," Richard said and they went back to his penthouse. He went to his office and booted up his laptop and started clacking away at the keyboard. Sylvia was very confused, but she had a feeling that maybe Richard was onto something.

Richard, being an accountant, had access to pretty much everyone's financial records, and he pulled up the record of Blake Fall. It seemed pretty normal for someone who was in prison and working as a waiter for a charity organisation, until it came to a transaction that took place just two days ago. A transfer from an untraceable account of thirty-one thousand seven hundred and eight dollars. That certainly wasn't a waiter's salary coming in.

The money had been washed through several fronts and that made the money untraceable, but Sylvia had another idea.

"Come, bring your computer."

"What for?"

"You'll see."

They got back to the station and Sylvia handed Richard's laptop to a forensics officer.

"Whoa. There's valuable work on there."

"Don't worry, it'll be fine."

"What are we doing?"

"Tell me, where do you do all of your banking?"

"In my office."

"No. I mean on what?"

"My laptop?"

"No! Everyone does their banking on their…?"

"Their phones!"

"Exactly."

Richard now understood. They could get the signal from his phone and track him with it, if he had checked that transaction from his phone.

It worked; they were now tracking Blake Fall's every move. After about an hour or so, they could see that Blake was at an old building that was scheduled for demolition, downtown.

"Perfect place to hide and store stolen jewels, don't you think, Sylvia?"

Upon hearing Richard's hypothesis, Sylvia smiled and got her tag team together. They headed to the building. According to the phone signal, he was still inside. They all got out of their cars to go inside, and Sylvia instructed Richard to stay in the car 'for his safety'. Richard knew however that what she meant was, 'so that you don't get in my way.'

"Do not leave this car, Castle. Otherwise, you'll be the new target at the department shooting range."

Richard paused and tried to think of an excuse to leave the car that she would accept.

"What if I have to pee?"

Sylvia looked at him and handed him her empty coffee cup. She left him in the car and went into the building with her team behind her and her gun in hand.

When they entered the building, most of it was dirty and in pretty bad shape. However, this was a good thing, as they could see shoe impressions on the dusty floor, there were many, which showed that someone had been in there frequently, and recently too, but all the footprints lead to the same room.

Sylvia pushed the door open and found herself in a room that seemed to be empty. When she and her team came to the point where they had to turn left in the room, they found a desk and chair, and they couldn't believe what was on the desk.

There, right in front of them was every piece of jewellery that had been stolen. Photos of all three victims. Tools for separating jewels. A map of the city, which showed the places that seemed to be the perpetrator's next targets. And most notably, and most horrifyingly, a human finger, in a jar of water. The finger still had a ring on it, and Sylvia realised, she was looking at Julia's missing finger.

That was the icing on the cake. They now knew, they had their man. All they had to do was find him. As Sylvia looked down the passageway, beside the desk, she saw Blake. Blake saw her, dropped the papers he was carrying and ran down the passage, where he grabbed a gun. He fired a few shots and tried to flee the scene.

Richard, still in the car, got bored at decided to sit behind the wheel. He pretended to talk into the car's radio mic, and acted out as if he was a real cop. He was enjoying himself.

At the same moment, Blake, still attempting to flee, knew he could not go down all six flights of stairs, or the police would catch him for sure. When he got to the second floor, he decided to try and put more distance between himself and the police chasing him. He charged into the window and jumped through it.

Richard was now pretending to be involved in a high-speed chase in the car. He was also singing a tune from an action movie with his eyes closed, trying to escalate the feeling, since the car wasn't moving. His song was interrupted by the sound of a loud bang in front of him. It was Blake, who had just landed on the bonnet of the car. Richard saw him and noticed the gun in his hand. He was scared, and resorted to something to try and incapacitate Blake. He turned on the windshield wipers.

He did not know what he was hoping or expecting to happen,

as the blades only smacked his face a bit but pushed him off the car's bonnet. He was now very agitated, and he still needed to escape, so he pulled his gun on Richard and forced him out of the car.

"She told me to stay in the car."

That was Richard's only excuse, but Blake opened the door and forced him out. He threw Richard to the ground and aimed at him. Richard, now fearing for his life, kicked him to the ground, got up and ran for cover behind the car. Richard did not make it though, as Blake caught his leg, and Richard landed on the floor too.

Blake looked in front of him, to his gun, which was within his reach. He grabbed it, but found himself letting go a second later, as Sylvia was now standing on his wrist.

"Go ahead. I need the practice," Sylvia said, as she aimed at his head, daring him to pick up the gun. Blake did not, and was arrested then and there. Richard got up from the floor and looked at her.

"I really tried to stay in the car. I really did."

"I know, Richard. Come on."

They drove back to the station and Blake found himself in the same place he was a few hours before. The interrogation chair, cuffed to the table. This time, he could not leave, because the charge had been laid. Many charges in fact, and he could not explain his way out of any of them.

"We just need to know one thing, Blake."

"And what is that, Detective?" Blake asked in a voice of despair, from being caught.

"Why did you do it?"

Richard then joined in by saying, "It wasn't for the money, so what was it for?"

Blake looked up at them, and considered his thoughts. He had nothing to lose. He was already looking at life in prison, with the number of charges laid against him. So, he decided to tell his story.

"I wanted someone to have sex with." Sylvia and Richard did not understand.

"I don't understand, Mr Fall."

"When I got out of prison, I wanted to have sex. But first I needed a job, and I found one as a waiter. That's when I met Julia. She was so beautiful and I thought she was perfect. But when I made a move on her that night, she rejected me."

Richard then began to tell the story along with him, guessing what happened.

"And my guess is, it was the same with Henley and Molly that night."

"Yeah. They rejected me too. Now, I do not take rejection well, or at least that's what the psychiatric analyst said to me in prison. So that night, I followed Julia home, and I killed her. I took the jewels, to make it seem like the killer's motive was robbery. Then later that night, I realised I could make good money off the jewels, and I needed money too, so I stashed them in that building. Next day, I went to work and I managed to get the addresses of the other two women."

"And then you went and did the same to them."

"Yeah, I got my revenge for the rejection and I took their jewellery, but now they were more like… trophies. And a means of finance."

Sylvia, now hearing the whole story was shocked and appalled. Three people were now dead. Their families grieving, and all simply because they rejected a waiter's invitation to have sex with him. She left the room then and there.

She now realised just how much pain rejection could cause someone, and what it could get them to resort to. None the less, she was satisfied that the killer was off the streets and people were safe. With the number of charges laid against him, he wouldn't be getting bail, or any parole when he was sentenced. He was looking at life in prison.

That afternoon, Richard had gone home and was cooking for Yvonne and Nathalie, when someone rang the doorbell. Yvonne answered and it was Sylvia. Yvonne invited her in to join them for dinner. Sylvia explained that she had only come to return her necklace. Yvonne then told her that she and Nathalie wanted her to tell them about the previous night, as they had only heard Richard's version, and he only told the good parts. Sylvia then agreed to stay and tell them the story. They enjoyed dinner together and once Sylvia was done telling the story, she told Richard that Blake would only stand trial in seven months, and that she would be in touch when there was another case for them to work.

Later that night, Sylvia lay in her bed, and thought to herself. *Rejection.*

She had never been rejected by anyone before, but she had rejected others before, and she was grateful that she was still breathing after doing so, as Julia, Henley and Molly had rejected someone, and paid for it, with their lives.

Chapter 8

That night, Richard sat at his desk with his laptop, typing notes to the case. As he clacked away at the keys… something struck him. He noticed something. All of the past three cases he had worked with Sylvia had something in common…

They were all based on love.

An idea ignited in his brain and he had a brilliant idea. He quickly shut the file he was working on and opened a new one. He had a brilliant idea for a new book. Even though he was halfway done with his current one, this idea was too good to just cast aside. He began to work on his new book immediately. And he had the perfect title for it.

Hell hath no fury like a broken heart.

He sat at his desk all night working, thinking to himself about love. It is like fire. There is beauty and good in it, such as the warmth it provides. But there is also great danger in it, such as fire can cause great harm and destruction.

The next thing he knew, he was being woken up by Nathalie. It was morning, and time to take her to school. As he got dressed and prepared to take her to school, he had one major thought on his mind. He needed to make his move on Sylvia soon. Time… was not on his side.

As he returned home, he received a call from Sylvia. "A new case already?"

"No. I'd like to know what you are doing right now?"

"Uhhhhmmm… driving home. Why?"

"Come by the station. We have a score to settle."

She hung up without another word. Richard was quite confused. It sounded like he had done something wrong. But if he had, he wasn't aware of it. He arrived at the station and found her waiting for him outside. She instructed him to follow her. He was intrigued, and confused, but followed her gladly. She led him to the shooting range room.

"Let's see who the better shot is."

Richard's eyes lit up. He now understood that Sylvia was still embarrassed by the fact that he had proven to be a better shot than her a few nights earlier. He picked up some safety goggles and earmuffs, then stood beside her.

"Oh, one more thing. We took your advice and improved the targets."

"Improved... My ad... what?"

Richard was caught off guard and a few minutes later, he understood. As the targets popped up, they began to move around. He then recalled what he had said that night.

"Wouldn't it be more challenging if the target was moving?"

"Me and my big mouth," Richard said aloud to himself.

Sylvia took out her gun and aimed. She fired. It missed. She fired again, and again, and again at least twenty times, and did not hit the target once. Richard giggled and Sylvia handed him the gun and he tried. He too had no luck. They took turns shooting and eventually Richard hit the target in the head zone.

"Ho ho ho... tell me you saw that!" he said to Sylvia arrogantly.

Sylvia did not want to admit that she had just lost to him, and fortunately did not have to, as her phone rang.

"Beckette."

Richard was curious to know who was calling and took off

his earmuffs to see if he could hear who was on the other side. He did not even get the chance to hear anything when Sylvia said, "I'm on my way."

She hung up and looked to Richard. "We've got a case."

She took off her protective gear and headed to the exit when Richard obnoxiously said, "Oh, let's hope it's another crime of passion."

Sylvia stopped and turned to him, shocked and appalled by what he had just said.

"'*Hope?*' Richard, we do not *hope* for people to be murdered."

"Okay, maybe 'hope' was too strong a word. It's just that, I'm exploring an angle of passionate crime for my book, so…"

They left in Sylvia's car and headed to the crime scene. A house on Flavian Street. When they got there, they could see one thing very easily. Whoever their victim was, they were pretty wealthy.

They went downstairs, to the basement where crime scene investigators were already at work. There was a very pleasant smell in the air, which was unusual. Normally a crime scene makes one's stomach tight and feel like throwing up. It was a smell that anyone could easily identify. Roses. Richard began to get excited. Since roses are usually associated with love, it seemed like another crime of passion.

When they got to the basement floor, they saw the body of a young woman hanging out of the washing machine. Sophia gave them what little she had found out.

"Single gunshot to her heart. She was killed instantly." Sylvia waited and turned to Sophia.

"That's it?"

"Yep. That's all I got."

"You usually get way more than that."

"What can I say? The body was washed in the washing machine after she was killed. Pretty much all other evidence was washed away.

There's no bullet. No fibres. No foreign DNA. Nothing. I'll only find out more down at the lab."

Sylvia looked frustrated. It was a bad start to an investigation.

"It looks like it was a professional hit. So, sorry 'Castle'. It's not a crime of passion."

As she looked up to Richard, she could see he was slightly distraught. It was puzzling to her. He had seen crimes scenes much worse than this.

"What smells like roses?"

"The detergent."

Sylvia walked around the naked body on the floor.

"Any identification?"

"Nope. We couldn't find anything. No credit cards, no driver's license, nothing."

"Then he probably took them with him. Let's get her down to the lab. Richard, you and I need to try to identify her."

"Oh, there's no need."

Sylvia looked at him and tried to figure out what he meant.

"I know who she is."

Sylvia looked at him, with her eyes widened.

"Now I understand why you've been so unusually quiet. Who is she?"

"Samantha Sullivan."

"How do you know?"

"She was a fellow novelist."

The silence in that moment was cold. They all returned to

the station and began to work. They confirmed that the woman was indeed Samantha Sullivan. A fairly low-rated novelist in the genre of romance. Richard then explained that they had crossed paths in the past, as well. It was quite a frustrating start to a case. No evidence. No suspects.

Nothing.

When the autopsy was done, Sophia informed them that she had been raped; however, that information was useless as the DNA from the semen had been contaminated by the chemicals of the detergent. There was one significance to it though.

"Something is interesting about it though."

"Which is…?"

"Seems that the rape took place *after* she was dead."

Sylvia and Richard were stunned. They went to their desk and thought. Soon an officer came up to them and said, "Detective. You might want to take a look at this" and handed her a case file. It was titled, "Jessica Sullivan." Samantha's mother. They went through it and discovered that Samantha's mother was a renowned business owner, until about six weeks ago when she was killed by a single gunshot to her heart, and her body washed in her washing machine, in Brooklyn.

"Same MO for the cases of the mother and the daughter? That can't be a coincidence," Richard stated.

They now had a feeling that someone was trying to kill the Sullivan family. But there were a few things that did not make sense. Firstly, they weren't much of a family. It was just Samantha and her mother. Her father had died just before Samantha was born, in a car accident. As for their extended family, they had disowned Jessica when she was just twenty-two, for selling a secret family recipe to prepare peanuts, so she could buy into a franchise.

Secondly, no one stood to gain anything from Samantha's death. She had no spouse, no children or anything. It seemed odd to hire a professional killer to kill someone when you won't benefit from it in any way.

Lastly, there was one large difference between the two murders. Samantha was raped after she was killed. Jessica was not. That suggested that the killer knew Samantha personally.

The case was really off to a bad start. As Sylvia and Richard got ready to leave the station, Richard noticed something. The house that Samantha was killed in...

"She was not shy about spending the money she got from her mommy's death," Richard said.

"How can you tell?" Sylvia asked, surprised.

"Sam was not a very good writer. How do you think she could have afforded that house we found her in?"

Once again, Richard proved he was good at finding twists and gaps in stories. When they got back to the station the next morning, an officer gave them Samantha's banking statements for the past two months.

They found that she was very broke, until about three days after her mother's murder, when her life insurance paid out three million dollars to her. Just two days later, she spent one point seven million on the house.

"Coincidence?"

"No way."

They also found something interesting. She also transferred forty thousand dollars to an account that was not registered to a business, but an individual by the name of Kyle Palmer.

"That's a lot of money to just give someone," Richard said.

They then learnt that Kyle was Samantha's most recent ex-boyfriend. It seemed that the investigation was finally setting sail.

"Let's go visit him."

"Agreed."

They went to visit Kyle at his house, which was about twenty-five miles away. When they arrived, they knocked on the door and were greeted by a rather muscular young man.

"Mr Palmer?"

"Yes."

"Detective Sylvia Beckette. I'd like to ask you something about your ex-girlfriend."

"All right, come in."

They walked in behind the man and into his house. They sat in the living room, and Sylvia began to ask about where he was on the day of Samantha's murder. The man got very confused; he was surprised enough when he heard about murder but the thing he found very confusing was the name of which she spoke.

"Samantha? Who is that?"

"Your ex-girlfriend."

"I've never heard of her."

"Really?"

"Yes."

Richard then did his usual and butted in with his questions.

"Then why did she give you forty thousand dollars?"

"What?"

"Her transaction history shows that she transferred forty thousand dollars into the account of a Mr Kyle Palmer."

The man then sat back and laughed to himself. "Oh, Kyle."

Sylvia looked at him and said in a slightly confused tone, "I thought you said you were Mr Palmer?"

"I am. I'm Mr Eric Palmer. Kyle is my twin brother."

"Where is he?"

"He left for Washington DC, last week. For a business conference."

Richard and Sylvia exhaled heavily. This was now a dead end if he was already out of New York last week, he couldn't be the killer. Later, at the station, they confirmed that he had been in Washington for the past week, by tracking his phone's GPS. So, with that, they were back to square one. No suspects, no leads.

A few hours later, Mr Johnson called them to his office. They figured it was because of the slow case they were currently on. How wrong they were? When they entered his office, they found him standing with two other men.

"Detective Beckette, Richard, meet Anthony Harris and Peter Thomas. They are our new junior detectives."

"New Jun... What... Why?"

"Well, city council figured that with the number of murders that have happened in the city over the past few weeks, we could use some additional detectives."

He sent them all out of his office and they all went to work. Peter and Anthony began to talk to Richard as they walked to their desks.

"Mr King?"

"Yes."

"I... I'm a huge fan and... will you sign my arm?"

"And mine?"

Sylvia got frustrated and turned back to them all. *'Oh, great! Now I have to put up with three idiots,'* Sylvia thought to herself.

"What is this, the Richard 'Castle' King fan club? We've got work to do."

The three men walked behind her and began to whisper to each other about Sylvia.

"Is she always like this?"

"Pretty much."

"She should loosen up a bit."

Sylvia turned around angrily. She pointed out that she could hear them and said that she'd loosen up their eyeballs if they were not careful.

"All right. So, what we got?"

"What do you mean?"

"I mean what is the current case we're supposed to be working on."

Sylvia gave them the lowdown on the case. Anthony then immediately asked, "Have you spoken to any of her friends?"

Sylvia and Richard looked at each other and felt like total amateurs. They should have been talking to her friends to find out about other angles for the case.

"But we don't know who any of her friends were," Sylvia said to them, in an attempt to try and make herself appear less stupid. Richard pulled out his phone and within a minute he said, "We do now."

He had just gone onto Facebook and found Samantha's page. Sylvia now felt even more stupid and nearly wanted to strangle Richard. They found out, through Facebook, that Samantha had a best friend by the name Rachel Bryant. And even more interesting, at least to the three men, she was a local prostitute.

That night, Richard and Sylvia drove around, trying to find her. They asked other prostitutes that they found and eventually, they were led to Rachel. They found her with a man in a suit outside a carwash. When Sylvia spoke to her and showed her police badge to her, the man turned, went to his car and left.

"Thank you, Detective. Now I've just lost a high-paying client."

"You've lost more than that recently," Richard said.

"What are you talking about?"

They realised that she had no idea that Samantha was dead. When they told her, she was shocked and began to cry. They asked her if she knew of anyone that wanted Samantha dead. She told them that no one would have anything to gain from her death. Richard and Sylvia were already aware of this.

Rachel than asked if they could take her home so that she could think. When they arrived, they sat together in her living room. That is when they told Rachel about *how* Samantha had been killed, and that it seemed professional, she had a possible clue for them.

"I remember something."

"What is it?"

"About three weeks ago, Samantha told me about a woman called Casandra Owens."

"What did she say about her."

"She said she was harassing her to sell her one of the companies that she had inherited from her mother. She and her mother were negotiating the sale of one of her businesses just before she passed away, and now Samantha was refusing to sell it to her."

That was the first real break in the case. They now had a good suspect. And given that it seemed to be a professional killing, it made perfect sense. Richard and Sylvia left Rachel to grieve the loss of her best friend and went home.

The next day they went off to visit Ms Casandra Owens. When they got to her office, her secretary said that she would be in soon, and so they waited. As they sat in the lobby, Richard was thinking to himself. They now had a pretty good suspect but he thought to himself, *'even with Samantha dead, it wouldn't help her to get the business she was trying to buy.'* He shared his thought with Sylvia and she agreed. About ten minutes later, they knew they were wasting their time when they met Casandra. She was very shocked by the news and her demeanour alone showed that she was not capable of murder.

Nevertheless, they had to ask if she knew anything. Naturally, she denied knowing anything and put them back at square one. Asking, who would have wanted Samantha dead?

Back at the station Anthony and Peter were also scratching their heads trying to find anything that could help them, but they were swimming in failure.

It came to the end of the day and they were no closer to the killer than they were when they discovered the body.

When Richard got home, he prepared supper for Yvonne and Nathalie. After dinner, Richard went to his desk and continued to work on his new book, "Hell hath no fury like a broken heart." Soon Nathalie came in and he asked if she had finished her homework. Being a cliché father did not suit him, and Nathalie pointed it out to him. He had to agree.

They had a fun few minutes of father-daughter time and then Nathalie went to bed, leaving her father to his thoughts. As he sat there typing, he had a thought. Both Samantha and her mother seemed to have the same killer. But there was one big difference. Her mother was not raped and Samantha was. He thought that maybe it meant that the mother's murder was professional and Samantha's was more personal than it looked.

As he thought about it more deeply, he realised that the only one with motive to kill Jessica was Samantha. She was the only one who would have stood to gain anything, and as they had found out earlier, Samantha was not shy to spend the money she got from her mother's death. But it was obvious that she couldn't have killed herself the same way she had killed her mother, then raped herself and washed her own body in the washing machine. Then it hit him. What if she had hired a hitman to kill her mother? That was the only thing that made sense. But then why set the hitman on herself too?

It was a real brainteaser. He had a pretty good angle but there were still some pieces missing.

At the same moment, almost by telepathy, Sylvia was having the same thoughts as she sat on her kitchen counter trying to think of an angle on the case.

The next day, they arrived at the office at the same time and said the exact same thing to each other, at the exact same time. It was kind of weird, but it showed how in sync their thoughts were. They sat at their desk and asked Anthony and Peter to find out if Samantha had any contact with any hitmen in the past three months.

"How do you think an amateur novelist would have gotten in touch with a hitman?" Anthony asked.

At that moment, Richard and Sylvia's eyes lit up and they looked at each other.

"The Internet."

They went and got the hard drive from Samantha's computer, which was in the evidence room. When they went through it, they discovered that Samantha's computer had been infected with keylogging virus. A type of virus that monitors the keys you hit and in what sequence.

Usually, it is used to try and obtain people's passwords. They went through it and found phrases such as "Hitmen for hire."

It was clear that Samantha had been on the dark web, trying to find a hitman. But it did not seem like she had hired anyone, or put out a contract for her mother's murder. It all seemed like another dead end.

As they were about to return the drive to the evidence room, Mr Johnson called them to his office. They had a visitor. It was none other than Rachel.

"What can we do for you, Rachel?" Sylvia asked.

"I think I might have something of interest to you."

Sylvia and Richard looked to each other and asked her what it was.

"Samantha had a boyfriend by the name of Kyle Palmer."

"We already know that."

"I introduced them."

Sylvia and Richard looked to each other. They did not know about that, but they did not understand how it was significant.

"Kyle came to me one night and as we were going to his house to have sex, we ran into Samantha and they… well… they hit it off. You could see that he had really just fallen in love with her."

"How could you tell?"

"The twinkle in his eyes when he looked at her. That's where I left them that night. Then, three days later, Samantha called me and said, 'Thank you. You have given me a gift that can solve all my problems.'"

Sylvia looked at her and then over to Richard. Richard then took over and asked, "What problems did she have?"

"I… I thought she meant her problem of being lonely. But…" She paused and exhaled heavily then continued, "But I'm starting to think that she also meant her problem of money."

"Was Kyle rich?"

"No. But…"

She paused again and this time began to cry. She did not say anything until Sylvia asked her, "But what?"

"I'm starting to think that she was involved in her mother's murder." Richard and Sylvia glanced at each other and then back to Rachel.

"Wait. You think she had Kyle kill her mother?"

Rachel nodded and Richard went out of Mr Johnson's office and back to the desk, leaving Sylvia with Rachel, in tears.

He went to the computer and found a path to the dark web that led to a site for contract killers. Once on that site, he saw one of the killers who were currently ready to take contracts. And there was exactly what he thought would be there. The name Kyle Palmer. He printed out the screenshot and took it to Sylvia. They finally had a solid lead. They went and told Anthony and Peter to get one of the vans ready for a trip to Washington DC.

"Road trip?" Richard asked Sylvia.

She smiled and soon the four of them were on their way to Washington DC, to pick up Kyle Palmer. They got to the hotel he was staying in and arrested him. Richard noticed something about him as they headed back to New York in the night. Eventually Sylvia asked Richard to take the wheel and they eventually got back to the station and threw Kyle into the interrogation room and went home to freshen up and rest before returning to interrogate him.

Chapter 9

It was morning sooner than Richard expected, and he had not been able to rest at all. He was thinking about Kyle, the man they had just arrested. Something seemed off about him. Something was just not right.

As he threw on his coat and headed out that morning his phone rang. He was expecting it to be Sylvia, impatient to start the interrogation. It wasn't. It was his agent, Amanda Mendez.

"Amanda, hey. What can I do for you this morning?"

"It's more what I can do for you, Rick."

"What do you mean?"

"I bumped into your mother yesterday, at the spa, and we got to talking about how well all your books are doing. Even your first book from four years ago is still doing very well."

"Yes. So?"

"So, we thought that it may be a good idea to host an event in your honour on Monday night. One for the fans to see you, get their books signed, the works."

"Monday night?"

"Yes. I'm already organising the venue. You'll be the talk of New York come tomorrow morning."

"What's new there?"

There was a scoff from Amanda's side of the line and she went on to say, "Make sure you have a date then. I'll see you soon."

"A da… He…Hello?"

She had already hung up. Amanda knew that Richard was not one to come to one of his own events with a date, and that request puzzled him for that simple reason. Now he was a bit nervous.

As he rode the elevator down from the penthouse, he was hit with an idea. He knew just who to ask. Sylvia. But it would have to be soon. It was now Friday morning. He had to ask her within the next three days.

First things first though. He had an interrogation to get to. When he got to the station, he found Anthony, Peter and Mr Johnson sitting at a desk watching the monitor.

"Three guys sitting around a computer screen? I hope that's not porn, 'cause if it is, I want to watch too."

"It's footage from the interrogation room of last night."

"And?"

"Guy hasn't said a word. He's just been sitting there shaking."

Richard walked over to the interrogation room and looked at him. Sylvia arrived and came to stand beside him.

"Shall we?" She insinuated and walked into the interrogation room to Kyle. Richard came in as well, while Anthony and Peter stood outside the interrogation room, watching.

"Mr Kyle Palmer?"

The words did not seem to reach his ears. He just continued to stare at the wall and shake rapidly as he had done from Washington. Sylvia tried to ask him questions and he still did not even move. She eventually slammed her hands on the desk, which frightened Richard but still Kyle did not move.

Sylvia gave up and she and Richard went outside to talk. As they sat at their desk, Sylvia said, "The guy is good."

"You know, Detective, it's not unheard of that when twins

are born, one is… mentally challenged."

Sylvia thought to herself. He was right. It seemed that he was the dull one of the twins.

"There's no way he could have done it," Richard said, with confidence, to her.

"And you concluded this how…"

"Anthony and Peter said he's been like this all night. There's no way this guy could carry out murder. Let alone be a contract killer."

His points were well-justified. Something was not adding up. Either they had the wrong man or… well, something just was not right.

Anthony came up to them and said that there was something that they might want to see. Or rather, someone. They went to the interrogation room and found Kyle with one of the finest lawyers in New York.

Someone who was very good at getting people off the hook, with Sylvia. Almost her greatest rival. He insisted that either Sylvia charge him or let him go.

Sylvia had no choice. She un-cuffed him from the table and let him go. As he and his lawyer walked towards to door of the interrogation room, Richard looked into Kyle's eyes and noticed something.

"You're not Kyle Palmer. Are you?" Richard suddenly said.

Everyone looked to Richard, in surprise. Then, for the first time since his arrest the previous night, he moved his head, very slowly, and still shaking profusely. When he was finally facing Richard, he nodded, very slowly, to indicate that Richard was right.

"How can you be sure, Castle?"

"If I remember correctly, Eric Palmer had blue eyes,

Detective."

Sylvia's eyes opened in surprise and she instantly turned to the man who they had believed to be Kyle. When she looked into his eyes, they were green. Therefore, this could not have been Eric's twin. It was... his body double.

Richard was now having thoughts and Sylvia was too. "There is no twin. Is there?" Sylvia and Richard commented simultaneously.

They left the interrogation room and Sylvia instructed Anthony, "Bring up the profile of Eric Palmer."

Anthony clacked away at his keyboard and a few seconds later announced, "There's no such person."

"Let's go," Sylvia said as she hit Richard's chest and ran towards the elevator.

As they went down to the parking lot Richard said, "So, the guy lied to us. He was Kyle Palmer. And he played us for a pair of fools."

"Yes, so it seems. Let's just hope he's still there though."

"You think he's fled?"

"Duh."

The elevator reached the lower ground and they ran to Sylvia's car, put on the siren and raced back to the house of Kyle Palmer. When they got to the house, they ran to the house and Sylvia banged on the door.

"Police, open up."

Nothing happened and Sylvia had no choice but to kick the door down, and draw her gun. She walked in and found everything to be in order until she got to the bedroom. They heard the roar of a motorbike engine starting. There, outside, was Kyle Palmer, on a motorcycle, starting to make his escape.

Richard and Sylvia ran to the car. Sylvia started the engine, turned on the siren and gave case. They raced through the streets and eventually they found themselves on the interstate highway. Richard looked over to her as they raced through the highway traffic and said,

"Is it really a good idea to have the siren on?"

"Yes. Why ask such a stup—"

Her comment was interrupted by a loud bang. A bullet had just come right through the windshield of Sylvia's car and gone right between her and Richard.

"That's why. 'Cause he can see exactly who is chasing him," Sylvia thought to herself and had to begin to perform lots of manoeuvres, weaving in and out of the highway traffic to avoid crashing, the bullets from Kyle and keep other drivers from being hit by stray bullets.

"Take my gun, Castle."

"Why me?"

"I'm a little preoccupied with the wheel right now! And we both know you are the better shot."

She had just given Richard's ego a huge boost. He reached for her holster and took her gun, loaded it and got ready to shoot. Kyle fired at them again and it took out one of Sylvia's headlights. Richard stuck his head and arm out the window and fired back. He missed.

Kyle then fired again and it took out the wing mirror next to Richard. Richard took his turn and missed again. He then had an idea.

"Listen, floor the throttle and let go of it completely when I tell you to!"

"Don't tell me what to do, Castle!"

"Trust me!"

They looked into each other's eyes and Sylvia trusted him.

"All right."

"Okay, floor it!"

Sylvia put her foot down on the throttle and they began to gain speed dramatically. Richard stuck his head and arm out again, and aimed.

"Okay, let it go, on three. Ready?"

"Ready."

"Three!"

Sylvia slammed on the brakes and Richard fired again. This time, he succeeded. The bullet hit the motorcycle's back tyre and it exploded.

Kyle was sent flying off the motorcycle and rolled and rolled and rolled until he stopped. Richard jumped out of the car and went to Kyle.

"Kyle Palmer. You're under arrest," he said, aiming the gun at him. Sylvia came up to them, cuffed Kyle and threw him into the back of the car.

"Nice shooting, Castle."

"Thank you, Detective," he said as he handed her back her gun. "By the way, you owe me, now."

Later on, at the station, Kyle was facing a whole list of charges. Murder. Fraud. Shooting at a police officer and more. He found himself cuffed to the table in the interrogation room, awaiting Sylvia and Richard's questions.

When they finally came in, there wasn't much for him to say. "Why did you do it, Kyle?"

"What?"

"Murder your ex-girlfriend, Samantha."

Richard joined in and added, "And her mother."

Kyle grinned and refused to answer them. Richard then tried to read his mind and said, "Maybe you were just a victim of your own emotions. You loved Samantha at first sight, and because of that you were too open with her. You told her what you did for a living, killing people, and you just did not know that, at that same time she was looking for someone to kill her mother. So, when she asked you, she took full advantage of your feelings for her and convinced you against your better judgement to kill her mother for her. You went through with it, but then later realised that she did not love you. And you got angry. So… so angry that you decided that she was to meet the same fate as her mother. You then went to finish the job, and killed her just as you had done to her mother. You tidied up and it was just like any other job. Is that it?"

Kyle looked up at him.

"Are you a writer?"

"Yes. Why?"

"That sounds like a book plot."

"I'm Richard King."

"Who?"

"You… You seriously have no idea who I am?"

"Nope."

Richard was very flustered by this. He did not think there was anyone who did not know who he was.

"Okay. So, you are saying that isn't what happened?"

"No, it is not. Not exactly at least."

"Then why don't you tell us *exactly* what happened?"

Kyle looked to his cuffed hands on the table and then up to them. He agreed to tell them. He had nothing to lose. He was already looking at life in prison, with the list of charges.

"Samantha and I met one night, through her friend, who's a prostitute. When I looked at her, I… I knew that there was something special about her. Something that made me feel a warm, fuzzy feeling inside. I couldn't resist it. We went back to her place and had sex. After that we started talking and I... you're right. I opened up to her too much. I told her who I was and she then asked me to help her by killing her mother. I thought that if I did, it would prove to her that I truly loved her. So, I went through with it. Like a routine kill. Then, about a week later, she gave me forty thousand dollars. When I called her to ask what it was for, she said it was my payment for the job. That's when I realised that she was not into me, like I was with her. I told her that I didn't want her money that I just wanted to be with her, and she told me that she could never be with a killer like me. That's when I got mad. So, I stalked her, and found the new house she was buying. So, I went there that night, with all my normal equipment. I came in through the chimney and waited for her in the basement. When she came down I... I could not even look her in the eyes and so I just... I killed her, pretty much the same way I kill all my other targets. But when I walked over to her body, that fuzzy feeling came back and it urged me on to rape her corpse. I then did the usual, and left her spinning in the washing machine. I went home and thought to myself, that I'd be the first suspect when she was found so I went for a walk and I came across a homeless guy, who looked just like me."

"And that's when you prepared the twin brother story to feed to the police."

"Yeah. I invited him to my place and gave him some clothes and then I gave him my ID, and then sent him to Washington."

"But you didn't know he was mentally unstable."

Kyle looked at them, slightly confused and then admitted that he did not.

With his confession, their work was done and they went out of the interrogation room. They eventually went home, knowing that their work for this case was done. Anthony and Peter were the last two to leave and they went to see Kyle and found him asleep at the interrogation table.

Once they left, his eyes opened and he smiled to himself.

Using his tongue, he pushed out a thin strip of metal from his mouth. It had looked like braces to Richard and Sylvia but it was not. He spat the metal stick into his hand and used it to pick the lock of the cuffs that held him to the table. He succeeded. Then rubbed his wrists, and went to the door and used the piece of metal to open the door of the interrogation room. He then got out and tried to find his guns. He found them, on Richard and Sylvia's desk, in the evidence box and tried to find a way out.

All the exits were guarded, but he had an idea. He went to the basement and found only one guard there. He crept up behind him and hit him on the back of the head with his gun. He then took his uniform, threw it on, over his clothes and walked right out the front door, hiding his face with the police hat.

At Richard's penthouse, he sat on his couch, watching a movie with Nathalie, when his mother returned.

"Ah, mother, what is this I hear about you talking to MY agent, and organising an event for me?"

"What, I thought you'd like it? You know, to distress from all this police work you've been doing."

"Point taken. Oh, by the way, we caught the guy today."

"Oh, good. See, so now you can even see it as a celebration."

"Yeah."

"Would you like to see how things are going?"

"No, I don't think…"

"Yes!" Nathalie exclaimed.

It was two against one. Richard had to go out with them and see how things were going at the venue. They all went down to his Benz and they drove downtown. When they arrived, everything was perfect. Even Richard had to admit. That's when he remembered that Amanda had instructed him to bring a date.

"By the way mother, why do I *need* to bring a date?"

"Well, I thought it was time for my dear son to get ***back in the saddle***, if you catch my drift."

Richard knew exactly what she meant and hit his forehead. As they went inside to see the decor, Richard noticed a police officer walking up the sidewalk and take a turn into a nearby alley way. He did not think much of it and went inside with Yvonne and Nathalie. Inside was just as perfect, with very dim lighting and blood red decorations, it was perfect, and Richard was now actually looking forward to the event. All he needed was to ask Sylvia to be his date. Which was not going to be easy.

As they walked outside and to the car Richard caught sight of a man coming out of the alley that the policeman had walked into. He squinted and when he looked hard enough, he recognised the man. It was Kyle.

"Hey!" he called out and Kyle caught sight of him and ran off. Richard ran after him, giving chase. He told his mother and Nathalie to wait for him in the car and ran off after Kyle.

Kyle ran into an alley and tried to lose Richard. Richard continued to chase him and as he ran, he drew his phone from his pocket and called Sylvia.

She was asleep but could feel the phone vibrating from beneath her pillow. With her sleep visor still on, she abruptly answered.

"What?"

"I'm chasing Kyle Palmer. We are running towards Limoux Drive."

"What!"

She launched herself up and pulled her sleep visor from her eyes in shock.

"How did he escape?"

"I don't know. Look can we try and figure that out later and you come help me?"

"How do I know you aren't lying to me, Rick?"

As Richard chased Kyle, he finally decided to draw one of his guns and shot at Richard. The bullet missed and Sylvia, still on the phone with Richard, heard the gunshot.

"Are you all right?"

"Yeah. Just about."

"I'm on my way, Castle."

Sylvia jumped out of bed and automatically realised she had a predicament. She was in her lingerie. She could not just go out and chase a criminal in a lingerie. Then again, she was in a hurry and had no time to change. She threw on her coat, stepped into her heeled boots, jumped into her car, turned on the siren and sped off.

Richard was still in hot pursuit of Kyle. They ran through the streets and Kyle eventually turned into an alley. He then pulled some old crates, which were stacked up behind the milk factory, down, to block Richard's path. Richard jumped over them and continued after him.

Sylvia, still nearly twelve miles away, weaved through the late-night traffic. As she raced through the streets, she hoped that Richard was all right. She called in on her police mic for backup, but there were no units available. She was on her own for a while.

As Richard continued after Kyle, they came to a bend, with a metal gate. Kyle went through, and slammed the gate locked behind him. Richard jumped over the gate, when Kyle fired again, and missed.

Sylvia drove up a street and noticed Richard's car. Next to it, she noticed Nathalie and Yvonne. She slammed on her brakes and opened her window.

"Which way did they go?"

"Down towards Limoux Drive."

Sylvia put her foot down and raced off, hoping she was not too late.

Richard continued the case, avoiding the shots that Kyle fired at random points. As they ran past a hotel, they heard the sound of a siren. Richard smiled and Kyle grew stern. He made a turn down a back alley behind the hotel. As Richard reached the turn, Kyle, who had stood still at the corner, grabbed him and put the gun to his head.

Sylvia raced along the main street, and looked into every alley. As she passed the hotel, she saw the silhouette of a man. She stopped, picked up her gun and went into the alley. As she went around the corner, she found Kyle, holding a gun to Richard's head, and waiting for her.

"Let him go, Palmer."

"I will. For a price."

"What do you want?"

"Let me go," he instructed, as Richard struggled to free himself from his grasp.

"Now you know we cannot do that, Palmer."

"Even to save your boyfriend, here?"

Sylvia considered. She did care about Richard, but she had taken an oath as a cop. She couldn't let him go. As the silence stood, Richard caught a glance of pipe above them. It seemed to be a water pipe. If someone blew it, it would be the perfect distraction. But he did not have a gun.

He looked at Sylvia and using his eyes, told her to look up.

She saw the pipe. She knew what he meant. But it was too risky.

"Put your gun down, Detective," Kyle instructed.

Sylvia turned to Richard and saw him mouth, '*Trust me.*' She looked back to Kyle and said, "All right." She pointed the gun up and made it look like she was surrendering. She was now aiming at the pipe, but Kyle had no idea.

"Now put it down," Kyle said.

Sylvia exhaled and hoped that it would work. She pulled the trigger and Kyle was shocked, but knew she had not shot at him.

At that moment, water began to rain down on Kyle and Richard. Kyle closed his eyes, to keep water out of his eyes. Richard then slammed his head against Kyle's nose, and elbowed him in the neck. He took his gun and aimed at him. Sylvia came up and did the same. She cuffed him and the two of them walked him to Sylvia's car.

"Well, that turned out fine," Richard said, with enthusiasm.

"Yeah, well. I'm just sad you did not get shot," Sylvia commented, sarcastically. Richard knew that what she was trying to say was, '*I'm glad you are all right.*'

"Ouch! Oh, by the way you owe me double now."

Sylvia was puzzled. She could tell he wanted something in particular, and she wanted to know what.

As they drove to the station, Richard noticed Sylvia's thigh, since her coat had pulled back when she sat down. He then said to her, "What are you wearing?"

Sylvia looked at him and decided to show him. She took off her coat and sat behind the wheel in her lingerie. Richard and Kyle both looked at her and whistled. Sylvia then put her coat back on and said to him, "Now I only owe you one thing."

Richard looked at her and tilted his head and exhaled lightly. He could not believe she had just tricked him so easily.

When they got back to the station, the officers were amazed that someone had gotten out, and when they got the interrogation room, they discovered how he escaped, as he had left the thin strip of metal in the door lock. They took him to the holding cells and locked him in.

"Get used to it. You'll be looking at this place for a long time," Sylvia commented as she threw him in and walked away with Richard.

As they headed to the exit of the police station, an officer came up from the basement, in just his vest and boxers. Richard then understood, when he remembered seeing a policeman walk into the alley, where Kyle came out.

"Come on, I'll take you home, Castle."

They got in her car and on the way, Sylvia exhaled and said to Richard, "Okay. What is it you want?"

"What do you mean?"

"You said I owe you. I know that you would only say that if there was already something you wanted. What is it?"

Richard grinned and realised that they were about two streets away from the venue for the event his mother and agent were organising. He directed her to the venue, and instructed her to stop outside it.

When they stopped, Richard pointed to the place. Sylvia looked over but did not understand.

"My agent and my dear mother have organised this event in my honour. For me to sign books and so on."

"Yeah...?"

"And I need a date."

Sylvia's eyes lit up with surprise, confusion and a flush of other emotions.

"Oh, hell no, Castle."

"You owe me."

Sylvia inhaled strongly and put her head to the steering wheel as she exhaled. She had to admit, she did fancy being his date, but she was still trying to hide her feelings for him. Nevertheless, her heart wanted what it wanted at that moment.

"Fine, Castle, I'll be your date."

Richard smiled broadly and Sylvia asked, "When is it?"

"Monday night."

Sylvia drove him home and agreed to be there. When she left, and headed home, she noticed something. That night, she had proven to herself that she really did care about Richard, and deep down she knew, that one of her worst fears had come true. She had fallen for him.

When Richard got upstairs to the penthouse, he found Nathalie and Yvonne asleep. He poured himself some liquor, and went to his desk. He could not find the energy to type and so, he went to his room and fell back on his bed, whispering to himself, "YES!"

He was proud of himself. He now officially had a date with the love of his life. But he knew, nothing was set in stone. He had to make this move count. The two months were going to be up in a week. It was time to roll the dice, and hope for a double six.

The next day, he sat at his desk, typing out a scene that he was basing off the chase from last night, when he received a call from Sylvia.

"Missing me already, Detective?"

"Uhmm, no. I just wanted to know if you are coming in today. Or do you need time to recover from last night's ordeal?"

"I think I'll take a few days off. But I'll still see you Monday night, right?"

"Yeah."

Sylvia was sitting in the examination room, waiting for Sophia. When she arrived, she told her about the date she had with Richard on Monday.

"Good for you girl. It's about time."

"What do you mean?"

"Oh, come on. You two were made for each other. And besides, it's about time you loosen up a bit."

Sylvia looked at her and for some reason, she was glad to hear Sophia's words. She was looking forward to Monday, which seemed to be an eternity away.

When it was finally Monday night, Richard's mom and Nathalie suited him up and got dressed. They were at the venue nearly ten minutes early and found a huge crowd waiting outside. It was going to be a challenge to get in without being seen.

Sylvia on the other hand, had left the station early, went home, showered and was trying to choose a dress to wear. She was feeling slutty that night and decided to wear her most sexy dress. One that would make a statue feel horny.

She liked to be fashionably late and waited for a while before leaving. By the time she was outside the venue, Richard was being 'harassed' by his fans for him to sign their books, their chests and even their children. Eventually, Amanda called him to the stage and asked him to read a few pages of his first book to the audience.

Richard, feeling that he had been stood up, read and the way he read, he touched the hearts of his fans. He was nearly done when he looked to the door and saw Sylvia strut her legs and walk up to the crowd. His smile, bright as day light, was clear to everyone and he could not take his eyes off her, as he continued to read.

When he was done, he found her talking to a stranger at the champagne table.

"There she is, looking as gorgeous as ever."

"Hello, Castle. Sorry I was late."

"Tough day at the office?"

"Yeah… Something like… that."

The two were now standing face to face. They stared into each other's eyes and drew their heads closer to one another. As they stared deeper into each other's eyes, Richard saw a twinkle in Sylvia's and Sylvia noticed the same twinkle in Richard's. They brought their heads closer and like magnets, their lips touched and they shared their first kiss.

For them both, it was a kiss that they both wanted to go on forever. It was a moment that no words could describe. Like all heaven and hell were in perfect harmony. Like there was nothing wrong in the world for that moment. That everything was just perfect. A feeling that no man can describe in words, as there are no words to describe it accurately.

Only one very short and inadequate word comes close to that ultimate goal. Bliss.

Yvonne was at the bar area and Nathalie on the other side of the room, being questioned by other children how it was like to have Mr Richard 'Castle' King as a father. When they looked, they both caught sight of Richard and Sylvia, in the middle of the crowd, and smiled.

Nathalie walked through the crowd and behind her father and took his car keys. Richard felt it and knew that they were not expecting him to come home that night.

When the kiss ended, Sylvia and Richard went outside to Sylvia's car and got in. They knew they were both thinking of the same thing.

Sylvia put her siren on and raced home.

They both knew that that night was going to be one to remember, for both of them…

Chapter 10

They got to Sylvia's house and from there... it was absolute paradise. They charged through her bedroom door and began to knock over her perfume bottles and her bedside light. Sylvia raised her right leg, which forced her dress to slide down, revealing her freshly waxed and shaved legs. She pushed Richard to the bed with her right foot, still wearing her heels. She then undid the zipper of her dress, under her arm and the dress slid down her smooth skin and fell to the ground, leaving her standing in front of Richard in just her glossy black heels, a very sexy black see-through thong and sexy black see-through bra.

As she walked towards Richard, she stepped out of her heels and grabbed the waist of Richard's pants and began to take off his belt. Richard lay still, mesmerised by the slight sight of Sylvia's nipples on her large breasts. When she had removed his belt, she stood in front of him and unclipped her thirty-eight-D bra, and let the weight of her large breasts push the bra off her. She then went down to Richard, grabbed his hands and put them on her breasts, then ripped off his shirt and lay down on top of him and kissed him, as she helped him take off his trousers. She could feel his erection against her vagina, from her large breasts and succulent nipples which were now against his chest, and their kiss continued for what seemed like eternity.

Richard rolled over, so that now Sylvia was beneath him and he watched the sight of her breasts as they sank against her body and bubbled about on her. His erection grew stronger and he slid down her to her thong and gently slid it off her crotch and onto the floor. He lay his head against her shaved vagina and licked it, sexually, as he made his way back to her head, to continue the kiss. He bit her gently on her neck and then kissed her again. Sylvia, eager to get his penis into her, raised her legs and put her big toes into the sides of his boxers and pushed them off. Now they lay together, completely naked and Richard then went for the finishing move. He put his large, erect penis into her vagina and they both began to have their orgasms. Sylvia could feel his penis hit her cervix and she enjoyed it more than any man who had done so before.

They lay together, kissing, biting and licking each other, turned the room into disarray, until they were completely drained of energy, and they fell asleep.

Richard woke up the next morning and found Sylvia in his arms. He was so very pleased. He could not believe that he had been inside Sylvia Beckette. The woman of his dreams. He felt that all he had set out to achieve, he had achieved. It was a feeling greater than any other he had experienced with any other woman.

Sylvia was woken by the slight movements of Richard. She looked up to him and smiled.

"That was incredible," Sylvia commented to him.

"It was."

They lay still and stared into each other's eyes. There was something in their eyes that they could find no words to describe. Like so long as you looked into that person's eyes, everything was perfect. No one else mattered. For that time, you had no burden on your shoulders. For that short time, you were… **FREE**.

Richard then thought of a phrase, one he wanted to whisper into her ear as they lay there together. But alas, a fear prevented him from doing such. The phrase was, '*I Love You.*' The fear was that she would not utter the same phrase to him in return. He had learnt a lesson, before he and Sylvia had even met, one that was important and that he had never forgotten. Love and Sex are not the same thing. Just because they had slept together did not mean that Sylvia loved him, and that very fear was his downfall.

Sylvia looked at him continually awaiting the phrase, 'I Love You.' And it never came. She knew in her own heart that she did love him but she had a code. Shew would never be the first to utter the three magic words because a lesson she had learnt from a friend was that whoever says it first cares more, and if the woman in the situation cares more, that's when the man may eventually grow bored of her and have an affair.

It was a stalemate, one that would be their downfall. Richard had the opportunity to make his world perfect, with the woman that he loved. The woman who, like all others, was imperfect and perfect all at once. She did not have the biggest breasts, but hers were perfect. She did not have the brightest skin, but her complexion was perfect. She did not have the voice of an angle, but her voice was perfect. He had the opportunity to seal the ultimate deal. But the thing about opportunities is that you have to take them when they present themselves, because if you don't, they can vanish in just a matter of seconds. As it so did in this case.

The romance and ambience of their perfect morning was rudely interrupted by the sound of Sylvia's phone ringing. She did not want to answer it, she was having the time of her life, with Richard inside her, but she had no choice.

She answered the phone and it was just what they needed. Sarcastically speaking. There had been a murder. Sylvia could not say that she was glad, but she was not exactly upset either.

She knew that Richard's two months were almost up, so this would be the last case that they would work together, and she was hoping that before it was over, he would utter the three magic words to her.

"We've got a case," she said to him.

He pulled his penis out of her and they got up and looked at the room that they had practically destroyed. The bedside lamp, the curtains, everything was out of place, but that is what happens when two people with genuine feelings for each other have sex together. Isn't it? They had a bit of a problem that would delay them, however. She needed to get Richard home, so he could change before they went to the scene, and they needed to shower.

As Richard watched her buttocks bounce around as she headed the shower, he grew even more hyper-sexual and ran up behind her and grabbed her buttocks. They showered together, kissing and having sex again.

When they got out, Sylvia got dressed and Richard put on what was left of his clothes and Sylvia drove him home to change. When Richard got home, he found his mother and Nathalie still asleep, exhausted from the previous night. He quickly got changed, left some money on the kitchen counter for them to buy breakfast and went back down to Sylvia. They then headed to the crime scene, feeling about as good as you possibly can.

When they arrived, it was the most gruesome scene they had seen together. As they walked up to Sophia for a briefing, they held hands, and Sophia, Anthony and Peter all noticed. They knew what it meant. The two of them were now an item, just as they all figured that they would be. It was almost like fate.

"What have we got?" Sylvia asked.

"Dead woman. No ID yet, but... whoever did this, is clearly

sick."

"Yeah, we all figured the sick part."

They stared down at the woman's body on the table, in her living room. The killer was very vindictive and possibly insane. That was the logical conclusion. The young woman had been stabbed in the throat then laid out on the table where the killer unleashed his or her sick mind. Her eyeballs, nipples, heart, liver and, most notably, her ovaries had been removed and the killer had then left red rose petals all over her body, presumably to mask the smell of blood.

"Who would do such a thing?" Sylvia asked as she let go of Richard's hand and walked around the body.

"Maybe someone who seeks out victims to unleash their rage of heartbreak on and then black markets their organs? Oh, my good God! I have to write that down."

"Where do you get the broken heart part from?"

"The roses."

It was a horrifying sight. To think that there was a person out there who was capable of such tremendous violence was stomach turning. It seemed that the final case that Richard would work with Sylvia would be far harder than any case they had worked before.

When they got back to the station, Peter got identification of the woman, and it was a very curious profile, one that made the murder seem even more insane than before.

"Ms Elizabeth Miller, AKA 'Sapphire'. Held a master's degree in medicine. She was a gynaecologist at NY Hospital. Cleanest record you can imagine. No enemies, no rivals, not even a single ex-boyfriend."

"Wow, that's tragic."

"What is, Castle?" Sylvia asked.

"That someone who helped women on a daily basis dies such a gruesome death."

"Yeah."

"Oh, that's not all guys. She had a second life. She was, apparently, very slutty. She was a stripper down at the Milk Us Gentlemen's club, downtown, hence the stripper name, Sapphire." Peter added.

The three detectives and Richard all looked around at each other. They had a very interesting victim. One with a very mentally unstable killer. The question was, 'where do you start looking for suspects?'

"Castle and I will go to Milk Us, and see what we can find. You two go to the hospital and see what you can find out there."

"Copy that."

"Can I just ask you guys a quick question? Why is it called Milk Us?"

The three men looked at each other with big smiles. They knew the answer but they figured that it would be best if Sylvia saw for herself. Richard drove them to the club and when they entered, the name of the club seemed very appropriate. The strippers in the club all walked around and danced around bra-less, and every single one of them had a pair of reassuringly large breasts. Some strippers lay on the bar table and let men squeeze milk from their breasts and that's when Sylvia understood. Every woman who was a stripper there had big breasts, and so therefore the name of the club was Milk Us, to indicate that.

"What is it with men and boobs anyw…?" Sylvia asked Richard but when she turned to her side, Richard wasn't there. She looked around and then saw him at the bar already holding one of the stripper's breasts. She then looked down at her breasts and thought to herself that hers were nothing compared to the ones these women had, and it made her fell a bit insecure.

She went to Richard and pulled him by the ear over to her and took him with her to the manager's office. The manager was very compliant and answered all of their questions. He told them that Elizabeth was a very popular prize for their regulars and that she was very open to conventional and casual sex. She had slept with at least fifty of the club members, which did not leave them short of suspects but it seemed like too much do delve through.

When they got back to the station, Peter and Anthony told her that they had had no luck, and that her record at the hospital was spotless. It seemed that they were going to have to go through the fifty suspects they had, for a few seconds, until Benjamin called Sylvia and Richard to his office.

"Look if this is about my two months being almost up, I'm very well aware of that."

"Well, yes. This will be your last case working alongside Detective Beckette. But that is not what this is about."

Sylvia and Richard looked across to each other and got curious. "Then what is this about, sir?"

"We put the case into the database this morning, as per protocol and the FBI contacted us. It seems that there is a serial killer that they have been after, and they believe that it is the same person responsible for the murder of Elizabeth."

"Based on what?"

Ben did not even answer and handed them a stack of six case files to look through.

"There is an FBI agent on his was down to New York, he should be here tomorrow, to assist you guys in the investigation."

They looked at each other and went to their desk to look over the files with Anthony and Peter.

"Mr Colin Hunter. Murdered by arsenic poisoning. Had his

eyes, heart, liver, penis and testicles removed and was left on his dining room table, covered in Platycodon grandiflorus petals." Peter read to them with a puzzled expression on his face.

Anthony took his turn and read, "Mr David Barillaro. Murdered through cyanide poisoning. Had his eyes, heart, liver, penis and testicles removed and was left on his living room table covered in Tulip petals."

Upon finishing reading, he too had a puzzled expression on his face and gave Richard his turn.

"Ms Kristen Lopez. Murdered by fatal gunshot wound to her head. Left sprawled on her living room table, with her eyes, heart, liver, nipples and ovaries removed and her body covered in Nymphaea nelumbo petals."

He, unlike the others had a slight grin on his face, as he was getting murder ideas for his book. Last up was Sylvia, with the last two cases.

"Mrs Sara Weston. Murdered by blunt force trauma to the head. She had her eyes, nipples, heart, liver and ovaries removed, and was left on her kitchen table, covered in daisy petals. And we've got a Ms Clara O'Connell. Murdered by drowning and suffocation. Had her liver, heart, nipples, ovaries and eyeballs removed and left on her living room table, covered in peach rose petals."

The four were puzzled. Things did seem to make sense, and yet they made no sense at all, at the same time. Richard then broke the silence by saying,

"This is a very rare serial killer. Usually, a serial killer will stick to a pattern. I mean, when you have a murder tactic that works, you use it again and again, because you know it will work. This guy used a different method each time. Poison, gunshot, drowning."

"Yeah. These are the hardest types of serial killers to catch."

They looked through the files a while longer and found that each victim was killed in a different place. San Francisco, Chicago, Atlanta, Washington, Vegas and now New York. It was very strange. They did not seem to have anything in common, or know any of the same people, or even each other. But Richard's fine eyes gave them one important thing before they left that day.

"Well, at least we know that they all had one thing in common."

"And that is what exactly, Castle?"

"Profession."

Sylvia's eyes lit up and she looked into the six files and realised one detail that would get them into gear. All six of them worked in the medical field. That could not be a coincidence, but it was also very strange. Doctors save lives, why would someone want to take the lives of a group of medical practitioners?

It was a question that they needed an answer to, and getting it, was not going to be easy.

"You two, get me the records of all the patients that these doctors had for the last three years."

"On it."

"Richard, come on, I'll take you home. See you all tomorrow."

Sylvia drove Richard home and they shared a kiss, as she dropped him off. When Richard got up to the penthouse, he found Nathalie and Yvonne waiting for him, to hear the details of the previous night. They had a happy family night and when they eventually went to sleep, Richard went to type a note to himself about how wonderful the previous night had been as well as the horror of the case that they were now working. Next morning, he woke up first and prepared a huge breakfast for them and went off to the station.

He was not the first one to arrive, Sylvia was already there, reading the patient lists to herself. She informed Richard that she had found two patients that all six doctors had crossed paths with. It was bizarre. They worked across America. Why would someone come across them all?

They went through the files some more, while waiting for everyone else to show up. They had only two names, Margret Cooper and Alison Perry. But it was strange. They were both born in New York and moved away over the years. It seemed strange to meet a doctor three years ago and the then come back three years later, just to kill them. But it was all they had.

When Anthony and Peter arrived, Sylvia ordered them to pull up the records of their two suspects. Before they returned, Sylvia and Richard were called to Mr Johnson's office. They both knew what it meant. The FBI agent who would be working with them had arrived. When they got to his office, no one could have predicted what was about to happen.

"I take it this is about the agent who will be assisting us, sir?"

"Yes. But if I am correct, you guys will not need to be introduced to each other."

"What do you mean?"

Sylvia and Richard stood anxiously and watched as the man sitting in the chair, facing away from them began to spin round. When they saw his face, they could not believe who they were looking at. **Dylan Anderson**. Their old school mate, and the guy who Sylvia had chosen over Richard eight years ago. He was standing before them and they would have to work with him.

Instantly. Tension. Began. To. Brew.

Well, sort of one-sided tension. Richard's sense of security was shattered upon seeing Dylan's face.

"Sylvia! Richard! It's so good to see you guys again!" Dylan commented and hugged them. For him, it was like a very small high school reunion.

"Likewise," Sylvia replied awkwardly. For her, seeing him was not the most unpleasant experience, but it was not exactly pleasant either.

"Good to see you, old friend," Richard commented, sarcastically. He was not happy in the least, but he had learnt to mask his emotions and he was very good at it.

"Now get out there, and catch this scum bag before he kills again. Now, get out of here," Ben said and the three of them left, to go back to work.

"Let's hang out later, and catch up. What you guys think?"

"Let's catch our killer first, and deal with catching up later, okay, boys?"

"All right. So, what do you guys have?"

"We have a connection between the victims and we're waiting for profiles on two suspects," Richard told Dylan.

"You guys have suspects already?"

"Yeah."

"Wow. I haven't had a single one since I got the case."

Sylvia and Richard introduced Dylan to Peter and Anthony. Anthony then handed Sylvia and Richard the profiles of their two suspects, Margret and Alison.

"Well, one thing is for sure you guys, Margret is definitely not the one behind this."

"Why do you say that, Peter?"

"Have a look, Beckette."

He handed her the file and to a detective, it was clear as crystal that she was not behind it.

"She's dead?"

"Yeah. According to that, she died of cancer, about a year ago. Oh, and she had a clogged heart artery."

"Well, she's a useless suspect then."

Richard on the other hand saw things from a different perspective. "On the contrary. It makes her a most promising suspect."

"And why is that, Castle?"

"Think about it. If she really went across the United States, just to try and save her life, and found that none of them could save her…? It gives perfect motive."

"She was already dead when these murders began, Castle."

"Not her… her family, her friends and whoever was footing her medical bills."

"What makes you so sure that someone was footing her medical bills for her?"

Richard gave her his look of, *'Isn't it obvious?'*

"Would you employ someone who had a blocked heart artery and cancer? Trust me, she couldn't afford that treatment by herself."

Sylvia, Anthony, Peter and even Dylan looked at each other, feeling really stupid. They had been trained in investigating and yet someone with no professional training seemed better at it than them.

"Peter, get me a list of all Margret's friends and family, start looking into them."

"On it."

"Anthony, what did you find out about Alison?"

"Alison Perry. Thirty-four. Clean record."

"Why do I get the feeling that there is more to this story?"

"Turns out that, coincidentally, she flew into New York, just three days before Elizabeth's murder."

"Get her picked up."

"On it, boss."

Now, the three old friends sat together around Sylvia's desk and talked, but Dylan cut it short.

"Well, guys, it looks like things are under control here, so I will leave you to it. I have to go and find a hotel to check into. So... I'll catch you guys later."

He left and left Sylvia and Richard alone at the desk. Sylvia noticed a very slight change is Richard's demeanour and said something that she did not know exactly how she hoped he would react.

"A stripper."

"Where?" Richard looked around excitedly for the stripper that Sylvia had just referred to.

"No. Dylan."

"Dylan's a stripper?" Richard asked with a confused and disgusted facial impression.

"No. I caught Dylan in a stripper."

Richard looked at her and began to understand what she meant.

"That's where we ended."

"I didn't ask."

"I know, but I thought my boyfriend should know."

"I'm your boyfriend now?"

"Aren't you?"

They stared into each other's eyes and got lost in time as they soul-gazed. They were about to kiss, when Peter returned and unintentionally interrupted them.

"Sorry, guys. Castle, your angle might work in your books but not here in the real world."

"What did you find?"

"Turns out that Margret Cooper and her whole family immigrated to Germany. Just a few weeks before she died. None of them have been back in the States since."

"So, a dead end?"

"Yeah. Where's Dylan?"

"He went to look for a hotel to stay in."

"All right. Why didn't one of you offer him a place to stay?"

"No!"

"No!" Sylvia and Richard both exclaimed simultaneously.

Peter looked at them, awkwardly said, "Okay," and went away. Sylvia and Richard tried to get their romantic moment back but it had been ruined by the suggestion that Peter had just made.

They sat together waiting for Anthony to return, for almost two hours and finally he showed up, with Alison. They were starting to get a little bit bored. It was strange, hunting down a serial killer who had eluded the law across the United States and feeling bored. They were two terms that you would not expect to hear in the same context. But it was only because of the things that they were thinking of doing with each other that they could not do in the police station.

They went to the interrogation room and spoke to Alison, hoping for slam dunk. A confession. But how often does that happen?

"Ms Perry. Do you know why you are here?"

"The cop who asked me to come did not say."

"Have you ever heard of the name, Elizabeth Miller?"

"Dr Miller? Yes. I used to be one of her patients. Why?"

"She was found murdered, yesterday."

"Mur…?"

She stared at Richard and Sylvia with her eyes open wide.

She was very surprised.

"Okay, and where do I fit into this? I last saw her years ago."

"We believe that you were involved," Richard bluntly responded.

Sylvia grew concerned. She had had Richard intrude in her interrogations before but he had never been so... blunt.

"Me? Involved?"

"Why did you come back to New York all of a sudden?"

"My mother. She was celebrating her seventieth birthday two days ago."

It was a very classic reason, but they had no reason to doubt her.

"Where were you yesterday morning?"

"I was at a local hotel. Visiting and old friend before I go back to Vegas."

Sylvia and Richard looked to each other. They did not have any reason to doubt her, still. But there was still one important question to answer.

"So, are you telling me that it is just a coincidence that you had been a patient with six different doctors and all of them end up dead?"

"Death is part of the human journey, Detective."

Sylvia scoffed, looked over to Richard and took out crime scene photos of the six victims.

"If they all suffer the same fate?"

When Alison looked at the pictures that Sylvia had laid out in front of her and gasped in horror. She knew them all, and was shocked and appalled at the deaths they suffered.

"Why did you keep changing doctors, Alison?"

"Uhmm..."

She took a few seconds to wipe the tears from her eyes and

explained.

"My bosses. They keep transferring me from branch to branch for the funeral parlour I work for. So, every time I was moved, I had to change doctors. You see I have blood pressure problems and lung problems and a slightly weak immune system, so I have to see doctors quite frequently."

"And so, it's just a coincidence?"

"Yes! I assure you I have nothing to do with any of these murders."

"Well, I'll let the hotel's security footage determine that."

"Can I go now?"

"You can go. Just don't leave town until we speak again."

Sylvia and Richard were not so convinced by her claim that it was a coincidence, but they would need to wait for morning to find out whether she was telling the truth.

They really wanted to have sex together again but they both knew that it would be best not to. At least until the case had been solved and Dylan had left.

Richard got home and went to his office and typed a disgruntled note to himself. He did not have to hide the fact that he felt threatened by Dylan's presence, to his computer. That day, Yvonne and Nathalie both noticed that he was slightly upset, but did not dare to ask. They assumed that Sylvia had pulled the old, '*It was meaningless sex*', card on Richard, and that would kill any man's ego. As they ate dinner, there was a knock at the door.

"Did anyone order more food?"

"No."

Richard went to the door and found that it was Dylan.

"Hey there old friend."

Richard had no response.

"Can I come in?"

Richard still said nothing. He let him in and when Yvonne saw him, she understood his foul mood. She decided to give them some space and took Nathalie to the bedroom.

"Wow. Nice place you have, Rick."

"What do you want, Dylan?"

"Well, I wanted to see my old friend."

"I am not your friend, Dylan."

"Aww, what is it? Still holding a grudge over the Sylvia thing? Come on! That was eight years ago."

"Never mind that. How do you know where I live?"

"I'm pretty sure everyone in this city knows where you live, Rick."

"I'll ask you. One. Last. Time. What do you want, Dylan? If it's nothing, then please leave."

Dylan took notice of Richard's hostility towards him. He left willingly, and as Richard closed the penthouse door behind him, he smiled with a malicious look.

He could tell that Richard and Sylvia had something going on and that Richard felt threatened by him. He then decided that he was going to have fun, and break them up, for his own fun and amusement.

Richard went back to his office and thought to himself, with his heart heavy. It was now going to be his ultimate trial. Like a duel of ancients, for they heart of the woman he loved. Sylvia Beckette.

One on one, and it could not end in a draw. He had to win. Or else it would be bye-bye to his dream of waking up beside Sylvia every morning, and having her as his wife. But he needed something first. The right mind-set. He was playing against the one man who had successfully defeated him before. He knew that deep down he was already afraid of losing again. He needed to get his confidence back, and impress Sylvia. He already had the fact that Sylvia had caught him sleeping with a stripper on his side, but he needed more.

It was time to change gear and put his foot down, if he was going to come out on top, this time around.

Chapter 11

The next morning, Richard woke up feeling determined. Ready to win the game. Once and for all. Like a rogue cop, who lives and plays by his own rules, he showered, got dressed and headed down to the station to get a head start.

His gut told him that Alison was telling them the truth, and with that they would be back to square one. No suspects. No nothing.

He expected to be the first one to the station, but found himself very disappointed, when he discovered Sylvia, Peter, Anthony and Dylan all there. Sylvia had a recognisable expression on her face, one that meant that she was a bit grouchy.

"What's going on?"

"Alison's story checked out. She couldn't have done it."

"So why are we looking at this board of names again?"

"Because, I'm sure that on this board is the name of our killer. I can feel it in my gut."

"Has anyone noticed that she gets a little bit cranky when she doesn't have a suspect?"

"But she has a point, Castle. The six victims have no other connection."

Richard knew that they were right. But they had not found anyone else who had visited all six. Richard then said something that got everyone's attention.

"I'm certain that it was a woman."

"And why is that?"

"Lining the dead bodies with flowers?"

"Yeah, good point. Plus, there is the fact that one of our victims was a gynaecologist." Anthony added.

"Yeah, but she was a general practitioner before that. She only became a gynaecologist eight months ago."

They all stared at the board with hundreds of names and after just about a minute, Richard's eyes caught something that he had a feeling would blow a hole through the case.

"Whoa! Whoa! Whoa! Look at this."

Richard got up and walked over to the board and circled one of the names under Elizabeth's client list.

"Jason Robert Lyman?"

"Yeah!"

"What about him?"

"Have you ever heard of a woman named Jason?"

"No. But we just said that... OH!"

Sylvia realised that it did not make sense. There was a man's name listed as one of her patients, after she had become a gynaecologist. It seemed that Richard, would once again be the one to give the case its kick off.

"But that name appears nowhere else, under the other doctors, Castle."

Richard knew that what he said was true, but he had noticed something that only a trained-professional could notice. Or just your average speed reader. He went and circled five other names, one under each of the murdered doctors and still, it did not make very much sense to the others.

"Jameson Ricky Lowell?"

"Jake Robin Lancer?"

"Jessica Ruby Lowville?"

"Judith Rebecca Larizona?"

"Jackson Rico Lacour?"

They all stared at Richard, looking very confused. He got a bit frustrated; they were meant to be good at this, but they were failing to notice what he had found.

"It's six different names, Castle? What are you getting at?"

"Look at the aliases."

They looked to the board and noticed what it was that Richard had noticed.

"JRL?"

Their eyes lit up. Now they all felt that they had something. Until Sylvia dragged the mood of success down with a simple comment.

"But it'll be impossible to figure out which name was real. If any were."

"Oh, no. It'll be as easy as learning to see."

"And how is that, Castle?"

"Wait and see, Detective. Peter, Anthony, would you please go get these patient files from the evidence room?"

"Sure thing, Rick."

Sylvia should have been used to these mind games by now, but she was confused.

"What are you going to do with them? Analyse their signatures?"

"Close but not quite, Detective."

She really hated it when Richard did this, because it made her look bad. The detective who is less intelligent than the novelist shadowing her.

But he had, almost always, been right with his hunches before, and also the fact that she was in love with him, got her to trust him.

When Peter and Anthony returned, they sat the six files

down on the desk and searched for the one document in each. When they had located the six dossiers and put them side by side, Richard picked one up and held it up, in front of Sylvia.

"Just get to it, Castle! Before I show you how my Taser works."

"Medical aid number."

Her eyes opened up so wide that they could have fallen out. She compared the number to the medical aid number of the other five documents. They were all the same.

"How did you know that she used a medical aid?"

"Just a guess."

Now they had something to go on with the medical aid number, they had to move fast.

"Anthony, Peter, run the medical aid number through the database. Find out who it's registered to."

"On it, Detective."

Sylvia, Richard and Dylan sat at Sylvia's desk for nearly two hours, waiting and eventually, Peter and Anthony came up to them and told them,

"Medical aid number is registered to a Jayden Remi Lott." Sylvia and Richard shared a knowing stare.

"Different name…"

"Same alias."

Seeing them so in sync shook Dylan. When a man and a woman finish each other's sentences, and share the same thoughts at the same time, it can only mean that there is love in the air.

"Did you get an address?"

"No."

Hearing Anthony's reply weighted the feeling of success, until he finished his thought.

"I got six."

They looked at Peter and Anthony with wonder and overwhelming joy.

"Six?"

"Yeah. You guys are going to like this."

He handed the three of them the document in his hand and they looked at it in amazement.

"No way."

"Yes way, Detective."

The document told them that this Jayden person lived in the same cities as the six victims, and all at the times that they died. Now that was too big of a coincidence to be a coincidence.

"Says here, this guy came down to New York less than a month ago."

Dylan, Sylvia and Richard all smiled. They had more than enough to have Jayden be a suspect. But something bothered Richard.

"Wait. A guy?"

"Yeah. Jayden is a guy's name. Isn't it?"

"Why would a guy be going to see a gynaecologist?" Sylvia gave Richard's question a sarcastic answer.

"Maybe the guy had trans-gender surgery. Come on, Castle. Let's go pick up this guy."

"Oooohhhh. Trans-gender. I like that twist."

The two walked to the elevator and went to pick up Jayden. Dylan watched them go and asked them,

"Aren't you guys going to take a team with you?" Peter and Anthony then said to him,

"Don't worry. Sylvia and Castle are the ultimate team."

In saying this, they agitated Dylan. He thought that they meant that they were dating, when in fact what they meant was that they could do great things together, as they did with Kyle Palmer. He began to think of how to tear them apart. Not because he was interested in Sylvia, but just for his own fun.

Sylvia and Richard drove to an apartment building, which was the last known address of Jayden Lott. They went to the woman in the lobby and asked her,

"I'm sorry ma'am, but does Jayden Lott live in this building?"

"Who wants to know?"

"Detective Beckette, NYPD."

"And this is?"

"This is…"

"I'm Detective Castle, NYPD," Richard said to the lady, lying.

"Yeah. It lives in apartment twenty-six."

"Thank you," Sylvia said and headed to the stairs.

"Whoa. Whoa. Whoa. 'It'? What do you mean 'it'?" Richard retreated to ask.

"Go up there and find out, Detective."

"Castle!"

"Coming, Detective."

They walked up the two flights of stairs and headed to the door with twenty-six on it. Richard was very puzzled. Why on earth would you refer to someone as an 'It'? It was very peculiar, but he knew that they would soon find out.

They got to the door and Richard decided to be his slightly childish self and said,

"Can I kick it down?"

"Another time."

"What other time? This is my last case with you."

"You cannot just kick doors down, Castle."

"Why?"

"Because if they are innocent then you owe them for damaging their property."

Sylvia raised her hand and hit the door gently, so as to knock, and then... the unexpected happened. It opened. Not because someone opened it. But because it was not closed properly.

Sylvia and Richard looked at each other, slightly freaked out by the door opening itself for them.

"Hello?" she called out. But there was no answer.

They entered the room and found a motherlode of evidence. There, in the living room were newspaper articles, about all the murder victims. With the words '*I'm sorry.*' written in red permanent ink.

Sylvia walked over to the bedroom and Richard went over to the book shelf, where he found a few of his books. He scoffed and then noticed another little table in the corner, with something nerve wrecking on it.

Sylvia, in the bedroom walked over to the nightstand and saw a horrific thing too. A pair of eyeballs, in liquid nitrogen. Frozen solid. Facing the bedside.

Richard sat at the little desk in the corner of the living room and found a gun case. Empty. Finally, he found, probably the most important thing of that day. An appointment card. As he picked it up and read it, he saw that the date was three days ago.

"Detective. You need to see this."

Sylvia, in her heels, ran to Richard and he handed her the card. When she saw what was on it, she knew that they had to move fast. They knew what Jayden did to doctors that he... or 'it' had visited, and the fact that the gun was not in its case... meant that he was going after this doctor.

"Let's move!" Sylvia exclaimed and immediately picked up

her phone to call for assistance. She called Anthony, and asked for him and Peter to meet them at the hospital that the appointment card was for.

Upon their arrival at the hospital, they questioned the receptionist about the whereabouts of the doctor that the appointment card pointed to, and she told them that it was her day off, so she had no clue where she was.

"Do you have her address?"

"Yeah. Here."

She quickly wrote the address down and handed Sylvia the small page. The four of them hurried to their cars and raced off. A person's life was at stake, and they needed to find this doctor, **FAST**, before she fell victim to Jayden as well.

They arrived at the house and found a car parked in the driveway, and another parked against the kerb. They ran to the door and found it slightly ajar. The four shared a look of terror and ran inside.

As they opened the door fully, they discovered that they were too late. There, in the passageway of the house, lay the doctor in her thong and bra. Dead. She had bled to death from a gunshot wound to her neck.

As Sylvia checked the body for a pulse, she realised that the body still had its eyes, heart, ovaries etcetera. Which meant that the killer was probably still around. And as she stood up, Richard looked to the kitchen entrance and saw a silhouette. The four then heard the sound of a piece of metal hitting ceramic stone tiles. The three detectives drew their guns and ran to the kitchen with Richard behind them. When they went in, they found a knife on the floor, but nobody was there.

They split up, Sylvia went upstairs, Peter went to the back entrance and Richard went to the living room while Anthony remained in the kitchen. They all feared the silence and moved carefully. Nearly eight minutes passed and they feared that the killer had gotten away.

As Richard walked back to the kitchen to regroup with the others, her caught sight of a table cloth on table near the staircase. He noticed that it was offset, and he knew that it was not so when he had previously walked past it. He looked under the table and no one was there, but there was a piece of pink fabric.

"Guys. Come check this out," Richard said.

When the others came, they looked around, but found nothing useful. Richard then caught sight of the control box on the wall and a framed picture next to it. It too was offset. That told him that the killer was still in the house.

He then had an idea. He used his arms to signal Sylvia to go to the living room, Peter to go to the Kitchen and Anthony to the bathroom. He then went to the control box and put his hand on the electricity switch. Sylvia understood what he had in mind and silently instructed them to as Richard said.

Once at their posts, Richard pulled the switch, cutting power to the house and he hid under the nearby table. As they stood silently at their posts, they heard the squeaking of a door opening. Richard then heard footsteps coming across the wooden floor. He then saw the silhouette of a pair of legs walk past the table and headed for the door. Once the figure had past, he got out from under the table and went to the box.

He pulled the switch up and yelled out, "NOW!"

As the lights came on, Sylvia, Anthony and Peter jumped out and surrounded the person. The person had turned around after hearing Richard yell out, "NOW!" and was now facing him. As the passage light came on, Richard was the first of the four to see the person's face.

"Oh my God!" Richard exclaimed as he looked at the person. His earlier question had been answered, and the answer was so unexpected, that no one could have possibly guessed the answer correctly, even for all the money in the world.

There, in front of Richard, Sylvia, Peter and Anthony was a person, with the face and facial hair of a man, and a pair of absurdly large woman breasts. As Richard looked down at the crotch area of the person, he also noticed that the thing had a penis. It was shocking, but it did explain why the woman at the apartment complex referred to the person as an 'it'.

"You're under arrest," Anthony said awkwardly as he cuffed the man-woman and the four took the person to their cars and drove back to the police station.

Anthony and Peter took the person with them, in their car and Richard and Sylvia went separately, in Sylvia's car. On the way, Richard commented to Sylvia,

"I guess the trans-gender guess was pretty close," Sylvia giggled gently and replied to him,

"Yeah. I guess. And… Nice work back there, Castle."

Richard smiled and put his hand on Sylvia's hand that was on the gear lever. Romance once again filled the air, and Richard wanted to say to her, 'I Love you.' But he couldn't. He was too afraid that she would not utter the same phrase to him. That the night they had together was meaningless sex to her. He could not summon up the courage to say it.

Sylvia also wanted to say it, but she did not want to say it first, and she too still feared that he would not say it in return to her. And so, neither of them dared to say it.

They arrived at the station, to find that Anthony and Peter had already arrived. The romantic atmosphere fell away as they got ready to do the last interrogation that they would be doing together.

They walked into the station and found everyone looking a little bit awkward, including Mr Johnson. They then saw Peter and Anthony come out of the interrogation room, and knew that the thing they had just arrested was waiting for them. It also explained the awkward atmosphere in the station.

They went to the interrogation room and Peter, Anthony, Dylan and Benjamin watched from the observation room.

"Jayden Lott?"

"Yeah." Jayden said, in a sweet, lady-like voice.

"We know that you know why you are here so let's try and make this quick."

Jayden, cuffed to the table looked down and inhaled, deeply.

"Why have you been killing these doctors?" Sylvia asked as she laid out photographs of the six victims.

"I didn't do it."

"Oh please. We found you in the house of yet another dead doctor, and you were getting ready to remove her organs with that knife you dropped in the kitchen. You expect me to believe that this is your first time?"

Jayden exhaled and looked down again. "How did you find me?"

Sylvia handed Jayden a sheet of paper with all the fake names that Jayden had used, with the same medical aid number. Jayden put her forehead in her hand and rocked his-her head from side to side.

Richard then used his famous way with people and asked Jayden, "What exactly happened to you?"

Jayden looked up and knew that he meant, how he ended up with a woman's voice and breasts.

"I was born like this. With a man's face, woman's voice,

man's penis and woman's ovaries."

"You are still a human, just like the rest of us, so that does not give you the right to take lives as you so please, and then desecrate their corpses," Sylvia said insensitively.

"Do you think I've been treated like a human, Detective?"

The answer was obviously 'No', but still, it did not make his-her actions right.

"How about you tell me why you did all this and confess, you could avoid the life term in prison if you do. Even if you don't, we already have more than enough to convict you, so you'll be doing yourself a favour."

Jayden sat still and shed a tear. He-she then said, "Do you have any children, Detective?"

Sylvia sat up straight in surprise. It was a peculiar question to ask. Especially given the circumstances.

"It's apparently the most fulfilling feeling in life. That is all I wanted. To have children."

Richard joined in and said, "But you couldn't."

"I have no fallopian tubes for my ovaries. I have no womb. I have no testicles. I couldn't have children."

"That still doesn't explain the murders," Sylvia said.

"I wanted to have children so badly, and so... I went to the doctors to see if maybe there was some kind of surgery that could turn me into a complete man or complete woman and..."

"And each of them told you that it was impossible."

"Yeah. Doctor after doctor, they all told me that if I wanted to become a fully-fledged man, I would lose my breasts and that even if they could replace my ovaries with testicles, it would be impossible to impregnate a woman with the sperm from them, and that even with the miracle that I could, it wouldn't be my child, but the child of the original owner of the testicles."

Jayden paused again, to take a deep breath. He-she began to shed more tears and continued the story.

"They told me that even if I could become a proper woman, there was no way for my ovaries to ever work properly. So... I... I got mad after receiving the same news over and over again, so I..."

"And so, you killed them."

"I thought that if they could not help me then... maybe... they did not deserve to have the thing I wanted either."

"And that's why you killed them and took their sexual organs."

"Yeah."

"And their eyes and hearts?"

"I... I wanted it to look like black marketers, who black market organs, and so I took all the organs that I knew how to... to take."

Sylvia and Richard looked to each other and shared the thought that Jayden was insane. There were now seven doctors, people who save lives on a daily basis, that had died and simply because they had told Jayden the truth, that he-she was never going to have children of his-her own. It was insane, shocking and appalling. But they had caught the one responsible.

They left Jayden in the room and went to their desk to regroup with the others.

"Well done, guys," Benjamin said to them.

"And Mr Castle, I guess... your time with us is at an end."

"Yeah. I... I guess so."

Richard felt a cold chill go up his spine. His time was up, and he still did not officially have Sylvia as his girlfriend, fiancé or wife. He still had about an hour before he had to go home, and he felt to himself, that he had to make his last move in that little time. But with Dylan, Anthony and Peter around, he did not dare to profess his love for her in front of them.

"Hey how about we go out and have drinks tonight?" Sylvia said suddenly.

"As a farewell to our dear Mr King."

"Why not? On who?"

"Me, of course, sir. It's my invitation."

"All right then."

Richard was surprised and he had a thought, the exact same that Sylvia had when she suddenly invited everyone out for drinks. They both thought that since it was going to be the last chance they would have to profess, they should do it when they were drinking, so that if it failed, they would just blame it on the alcohol the next day, and say they were drunk. It seemed like a fool proof plan.

The six of them, Ben, Anthony, Peter, Dylan, Sylvia and Richard went to the classiest bar in all New York, one where Richard was well known. They ordered drinks and Sylvia, feeling nervous about professing to Richard in front of her ex and colleges made one, just one tiny mistake that she would later regret.

The four men had their different whiskies and Sylvia surprised them all by ordering Vodka. Very strong Vodka. And the reason that this was a fatal mistake of that night, was because she had one glass too many.

She sat at the bar alone for a few minutes as she summed up her courage when Dylan came and sat next to her. They laughed and joked about many things together. The case they had just solved. Their old school mates. Their history. However, Dylan was slightly jealous of what Sylvia was doing for Richard. The amount of alcohol that the five of them had bought that night was extreme, and the fact that she was willing to spend all of that money over Richard was... how one would describe as overboard.

There was one big difference between the four men and Sylvia, however. It was the fact that she was now intoxicated and the four men were still sober. The thought of telling Richard how much she loved him was still on her mind, and in her intoxicated state she uttered the words, "I love you."

But she was not saying it to the man she intended. She was now saying it to Dylan. Richard, still sober, and sitting with the other three men at a table behind Sylvia and Dylan, overheard her, as she uttered the three magic words to Dylan. Dylan, sitting with Sylvia turned to her, surprised at what she had said, and thought to himself. He still wanted to hurt Richard and now he had a golden opportunity to do so. He looked to her and out of the evil within him said, "I love you, too."

Richard, hearing this, was torn in two. He now was experiencing a pain, deep inside him. A familiar pain. A pain that he had felt once before, eight years ago, when he professed his love for Sylvia to her. A pain beyond description. A pain so great that a knife through the heart would have seemed like a feather landing on your palm. A pain that no words can describe accurately.

Now, upon hearing her say this, he believed that the words were meant for Dylan's ears, and he believed that she had chosen Dylan over him again. The pain of that, failing with the person you love, not once but twice, is beyond compare, and it killed him inside.

Sylvia eventually went to the bathroom and Richard then went over to the bar and ordered more alcohol. He drank and drank until he was intoxicated and the barman had to call an Uber to take him home. Dylan sat at the bar and he could see just how hurt Richard was, and he smiled with maniacal delight that he had successfully broken Richard, again.

Richard got home and began to sober up, as he walked to his room. It was one of the few times where he wished that he was a woman. He was always grateful to be a man, as it meant he did not have to go through the process of giving birth, but the simple fact was that women do tend to take rejection better than men. The reason being that all men have an ego, some larger than others and his ego was absurdly large and because of that, his ego could not handle rejection nor the thought that there was a man who someone would consider better than him.

Something changed that night inside Richard. Something snapped. Something that no one could fix. His heart had been broken. Beyond repair. By the same woman who had broken his heart many moons before, and over the same man she had chosen over him before. But it had done something else to him too.

It had made him see Sylvia in a different light. She was no longer the ultimate woman to him, and she would never be the ultimate woman to him, ever again, because on that fateful night Richard lost something. Something that over the past eight years he did not think was possible to lose.

His love for Sylvia Beckette.

Chapter 12

The next morning, the sun rose and shone its beams brightly into Sylvia's eyes from where she lay, naked, on her bed. She opened her eyes to find that her curtains were open and that she had a massive headache. It was the hangover from all the alcohol she had drank the previous night.

She got up and felt a sharp pain in her breasts, the pain of them being full of alcohol. She lay on her bed for about ten more minutes and finally got up to her feet. She went to the bathroom, and did her morning ablutions. She then went to the kitchen to have her morning coffee and put a hangover pill it.

The previous night was all a blur to her. The last thing she could remember was going to the bar with the others, but she was unsure if she had told Richard how she felt about him. She felt quite foolish, for having the plan in place and then intoxicating herself to the point that she could not carry it out properly.

At the same moment as she stood, naked, in her kitchen, a powerful wind burst the window open. The cold wind was familiar. It meant that a heavy storm was on its way. The cold air blew through Sylvia's hair as she thought about what to do. She needed to find out what had happened the previous night. Did she tell Richard that she was in love with him or not? Did he say he felt the same or not? Those are questions that nobody likes to wait for the answers to.

That was the only thing on her mind, until the cold wind coming through the window started biting her vulva and nipples and prompted her to go and have a warm shower and get dressed.

Richard, in his luxurious penthouse, woke up and found himself with a slight headache as well. He was hoping and praying to himself that it had all been an awful dream. That Sylvia had not chosen Dylan over him again, but his clothes that lay on the chair beside his bed, wrecked with the stench of alcohol and his headache were confirmation that it was no dream.

He got up and looked out of his window. Storm clouds were approaching. He was unsure why he cared. He was still bleeding from his broken heart. It was unbelievable. That the woman he deemed to so perfect had just stabbed him in the heart. All over again.

Sylvia was a woman who he saw as flawless. One who was beyond compare to any other woman in the world. God's most perfect creation. At least this was so, in Richard's eyes. Until he thought to himself, *What was so great about her?*

He had no answer to that question. He thought harder and realised that he never had been able to answer that question. He did not know what it was about Sylvia that made her so incredible. She was smart, but he had met many other women who were smarter than her. She had big breasts, but he knew many other women who had bigger breasts. She had a bright smile, but there were many other women with brighter smiles.

When he was honest with himself, he had to admit, he did not understand why he loved her so much. Every quality that she possessed that he found attractive he could find in a much greater quantity with other women. His only answer, which he was uncertain of, was that the thing that made Sylvia Beckette so special was the combination, of her personality, sexual organs and talent. And that's why she was one of a kind. And no matter what he tried, there was no other woman like her, anywhere in the world. She was unique and there was no woman like her.

Then, Richard had a thought. He realised something at that moment. He realised that as he thought about her, he did not feel a fire spark burn, deep inside his heart. He then went to the chest, next to his bed and opened it with his thumb print. He pulled out and old photo of himself and Sylvia, together and when he looked at it, he realised that his feelings for her were gone.

He was still hurt, that she chose Dylan over him but it was her choice, and he couldn't do anything about it. It was then that he decided that the best thing to do would be to finish the book he had been writing. Once that was done, he would have no reason to think about the past few months that he had spent with Sylvia. Once the book was done, he could leave the past, and Sylvia, behind him. And be free.

He left his room, went to the bathroom, and cleaned himself up. Afterwards, he got dressed, ate some breakfast and went to his office. He poured himself some whiskey and sat at his desk. He soon was hard at work, finishing his book, and trying to forget about Sylvia.

Dylan, in his hotel room, woke up and rolled over, so that he was facing up. He had a grin on his face and began to giggle. He had succeeded at breaking Richard's heart, with Sylvia. He was proud of himself. As he rose to his feet, in his boxers and vest, he had a thought.

He came to a realisation. He realised that, even though his feelings for Sylvia were not as strong as they were eight years before, he still had feelings for her. He admitted to himself that he had been lying to himself, saying that he no longer had feelings for her. She was a woman beyond compare to him, and she had chosen him, over Richard, who was practically the most successful man in all of New York. To him that only meant one thing.

She loves me. Truly.

He went to the bathroom of his hotel room and pulled out his manhood, to drain his bladder. As he did, he stared into the mirror in front of the toilet, and smiled. His ego had gotten so much bigger, and he was happy. He had killed two birds with one stone. Richard's heart was broken and he had the woman he loved.

He had his morning shower, ordered breakfast from the hotel restaurant, put his suit on and headed out, to the New York police station. He noticed the storm clouds that were in the sky, and he did not care. He did not care if it rained elephants that day, because he had the woman of his dreams to go and visit.

Sylvia, still at her house, had a shower, got dressed, had a small bite to eat and headed out to the station. She was still trying to remember what had happened the previous night, but it was all a blur. But she was determined to find out.

As she parked her car, at work, a flash of lighting struck in front of her, and a loud bang of thunder pierced her ears, and the ears of everyone throughout the city of New York. The storm had arrived.

Sylvia went to her desk, to find that Peter and Anthony were waiting for her. They were bored, and playing rock-paper-scissors. They had nothing to do until there was another homicide.

Sylvia sat at her desk and eventually grew bored. She joined them and Anthony bravely, and subtly said to Sylvia, "So, Dylan, huh?"

Sylvia looked at Anthony. She was shocked and confused.

"So, Dylan what?"

"You like him?" Peter answered.

"What are you guys talking about?"

"You gave him the whole 'I Love You' speech last night."

Sylvia opened her eyes wide, in shock. She did not want to believe them. Had she professed to the wrong man?

"And here I thought you liked Castle," Anthony continued.

Sylvia was confused and scared out of her mind. She was now worried about Richard. How he must have felt. Or did he feel anything at all? He had never confirmed that he still loved her, after all.

Her thoughts were interrupted by the sound of the intercom. It was Mr Johnson, summoning her to his office.

"Sir?"

"Beckette. Please come in."

"What is this about, sir?"

"It's about you and your FBI lover."

His words pierced her ears. She now knew that it had to be true, she had professed, but to the wrong man.

"I'd just like to remind you that there is a strict policy about FBI agent and police officers dating. Especially when they work in the same jurisdiction."

"Yes, sir, I know."

"So, remember, if your relationship with him interferes with any cases, you'll be out of that door faster that you can say, 'Bing-bang-boom'."

Sylvia exhaled and explained to Mr Johnson that she was drunk and that she did not mean to say it to Dylan. She made it clear that there was no relationship between the two of them. Mr Johnson was glad, and let her go.

As Sylvia stood in the doorway of Mr Johnson's office, she caught sight of Dylan, with Anthony and Peter. She crouched down and made her way to the ladies room. She went and sat on the toilet seat and thought to herself.

Now she had TWO huge problems. Not only did she have to go and talk to Richard about her feelings for him, she also had to tell Dylan that she was not in love with him.

"What have I got myself into?" she asked herself and slapped her forehead. She sat in the bathroom for nearly an hour, thinking of what to do.

Firstly, there was the matter of Dylan. He did not seem like such a problem. She was planning to say that she did not remember anything, because she was drunk and that would have been a quick fix. But her real worry was Richard.

She was more concerned about Richard. She did not want to go to him, looking desperate, but she also did not want him to think that he was second choice to Dylan. She really had a lot to think about.

She finally noticed her hips and thighs feeling sore from sitting on the toilet for so long. She got up, pulled up her pants and went out, to speak to Dylan.

He was waiting to see her, with Anthony and Peter.

"Hello, Detective!" he exclaimed, and walked up to her, grabbing her hips. She went ahead with her plan, to make it seem that she did not remember what she had said to him the previous night, but Anthony blew it up in her face by saying that he and Peter had told her that morning.

Sylvia had no choice, she had to do this the more hurtful way.

"Look, Dylan, I don't know what you want me to say. I was under the influence."

"So?"

"So, I never meant to say that to you. We were over, years ago."

Dylan's eyes opened wide. He was hoping that his ears were

deceiving him.

"So... you're... you're not... you're not in love with me?"

"No! Definitely not."

Her words held his heart and her nails dug deep into his arteries. She had just pulled out his heart and destroyed it. It was a pain that he had never experienced before, but it was so excruciating that it felt as though he had been this way since birth. What was this feeling? Heartbreak.

Sylvia walked away, unaffected, and went to her car, despite the booming thunder and striking lighting outside. Dylan remained still for several minutes and eventually wobbly-walked over to a nearby chair and put his hands on his head. He felt so much pain within him, pain that he could not describe. It made the pain of a guard dog bite seem like little more than drop of water landing on your toe.

He sat by himself for a while and about an hour later he got to his feet and went downstairs to his car. A thought crossed his mind while he sat in his car. This pain he was feeling was the exact same pain that he so dearly wanted Richard to feel.

A brother shouldn't wish such extreme pain on their worst enemy, Dylan said to himself, in his mind. He could not believe it, and as he thought to himself some more, he realised that just twenty-four hours before, if Sylvia had said the exact same words to him, he wouldn't have cared. The reason he felt this way was because he had fallen in love with Sylvia, all over again, that morning.

The storm grew more and more violent, so to the point that a few trees had fallen over and people started to go home. Sylvia decided to do the same, before her car was blown over. Dylan on the other hand wanted to go somewhere before heading back to the hotel.

Richard sat at his desk, drinking fine brandy, trying to get over his broken heart. He was almost done with the last chapter of his book. The next day he would call his publisher, to start organising the cover art and launch event. He had one of his penthouse windows open, so he could smell the sweet smell of rain in the grass below. Nathalie and Yvonne were having fun baking a cake in the kitchen and all was harmonious.

In all the rain and thunder that the weather report said would last for days. The sound of someone knocking at the door broke through the all-natural noise.

Richard opened the door and found that it was Dylan.

"Hey, Rick. May I come in?"

Richard opened the door wider and let him in.

"What do you want, Dylan? You here to gloat?"

"No. Quite the opposite, actually. I'm here to apologise."

Richard looked at him, confused and curious.

"Huh?"

"You know… what happened in the bar. Last night."

"Yeah?"

"Yeah, well, she broke up with me today. Basically."

"Basically?"

"Apparently, she did not mean to say anything last night but…"

"Then… why… are you apologising?"

"Because, now I know how you felt eight years ago. It's a pain beyond description."

"Yeah."

The two men went to Richard's office and continued their conversation. Eventually, they began to drink some of Richard's fine brandy and beer. When the time came for Dylan to leave, he was too drunk to drive, and Richard had to call for a cab to take him back to the hotel.

Once he had left, Richard went back to his office and looked out the window, at the monstrous storm that was holding New York in its clutches. He took a sip from his glass of brandy, and got to thinking.

Sylvia, while she was amazing and was able to evoke feelings in men that even they could not understand, had an interesting superpower. She could break hearts and leave men in pieces, without even trying. She could rob men of their ability to love other women. While she was great at sex, she could use it as a weapon to lure her prey in and tear him to pieces in just a matter of days. She was a puzzle. But there was one thing she had done to Richard that he could not forgive, and now she had done the same to Dylan.

He realised that she could do the same to almost any other man she met. As long as she was breathing, she could do irreparable damage to many other men, equivalent or worse than that, which she had done to Dylan and Richard in the past twenty-four hours. He thought to himself a few seconds longer and came to a decision.

For the sake of all men everywhere. The safety of many hearts. The continuity of many existing marriages. The possibility for happiness of many other women. For everything that he wanted others to experience… Sylvia 'Becky' Beckette… had to die.

His thoughts came accompanied by a blue flash of lighting that silhouetted him in his office. His eyes and face shone blue in response to the lightning flash, as his evil thoughts filled his heart.

Sylvia's thoughts at the same moment were the Yin to the Yang of Richard's thoughts. She was thinking to herself, as she watched the storm and lightning from her window. She knew that while the current storm would leave many with the flu, and some buildings damaged, but she chose to see the brighter side of the storm. It would give birth to new plants and fill the rivers and dams with water for wild animal species to drink.

She thought of Richard. She longed for him. The night they had sex for the first time was permanently marked in her heart. She wanted to feel Richard's hands on her breasts, she wanted to feel his testicles and scrotum in her hands, she wanted to feel his large penis penetrate her vulva and rub against her cervix, but it was not just the sex, she wanted to hear his rough yet gentle voice utter the words that he had said to her eight years prior.

'I Love You.'

She thought to herself a while longer and decided to put her pride, her ego, everything aside and tell Richard how she felt about him. If he did not feel the same, it would be her loss, but she had to try. For her happiness.

She went to her bedroom and took off all her clothes and looked at her naked reflection. She pondered and realised something. She was not the sexiest, the smartest, the richest or the best at anything, but for as long as she could remember, the look in Richard's eyes, even eight years before, made her feel like the ultimate woman. He made her feel sexier than Megan Fox. It made her feel smarter than Marilyn Vos Savant. It made her feel that there was no other woman like her. It made her feel that she was the ultimate woman in the world. And he was the only one who had ever made her feel like that. Having a man that could make her feel so special was more important than her pride.

She decided to give herself a few days to gather up the courage and tell Richard how she felt about him, and all she could do was hope that everything would go exactly as she hoped.

Meanwhile, Richard was hard at work on the last chapter of his book, and thinking about how to kill Sylvia. He had learnt about how to commit crime from his years of writing, listening to cases in the court and from working alongside Sylvia. He knew about, virtually, all the little things killers leave behind, and that catch up to them later.

He had to use his knowledge to help him commit the perfect murder. He sat at his desk for hours and eventually a plan took shape. The first thing he needed was a weapon. He obviously could not buy a gun of his own because it could be traced back to him. He also needed a way to get Sylvia out to a secluded location, where he would not be disturbed. He needed a lot, and fast. The storm would last for several days. If he could do it in these conditions, it would mean less chance of being disturbed, meaning more time to dispose of the evidence.

As he shut his MacBook and poured himself one last glass of whisky for the night, the perfect idea came to him. He could make the case an open and shut case, by getting the perfect fall guy for the crime. Dylan.

Sylvia had practically just broken up with him. That gave him motive.

All he would need then, was Dylan's gun. And since it's lands and grooves were already in the Interpol database, the second they were scanned, it would point to Dylan's gun. It would not take long for the police to arrest him. The rest, he would still need to plan out. But first things first. He needed Dylan's gun.

He went back to his desk and opened his MacBook and immediately started searching the internet. He had an idea. If he could knock Dylan out for a few hours somehow, he could take the gun, carry out the murder and return it before he woke up.

He searched the dark web and after a few hours found a drug that could render someone unconscious for eighteen hours. It was odourless, colourless, tasteless and would still work perfectly if it was induced through any form of liquid. He ordered it and then tried to fall asleep, but planning a murder can really affect one's sleep patterns. He got up and wondered his penthouse, thinking of how to carry out his plan.

He had the perfect plan to knock Dylan out. He could just pour the drugs into a bottle of whisky, and give it to him. It wouldn't be too unexplainable, as they were now a little bit more like brothers, since they had both been broken hearted. But what about the actual murder? That was the question.

He walked around for so long that eventually he realised the sun was up. He went and checked his phone; it was eight o'clock in the morning. He had been up all night. A few seconds later, he heard his doorbell ring.

It was a delivery man; with the drugs he had ordered. Things were moving fast now. All he needed was to use the drugs on Dylan, in such a way that he could get everything done within the eighteen hours.

Richard made breakfast for the three of them and they had one of the few mornings where they got to enjoy their breakfast together. With the heavy storm, schools did not expect students to come and Richard was still on his self-approved leave from work.

When they were done eating, Richard went to his office and continued with his book. He was nearly done and looking forward to finishing it, when his phone rang. As he glanced at the screen, the caller ID showed that it was Sylvia. He did not want to answer it, and have to hear her voice again, but it would mean that the plan would move faster.

Sylvia, on the other end, had gathered up enough courage to ask Richard to meet her, so she could tell him that she loved him. She was still in bed, naked, and holding her left breast, uttering to herself, *'please pick up, please pick up, please pick up.'*

Richard exhaled heavily and answered Sylvia's wish. He pressed the green button and said, "Hello?"

Sylvia was so happy, she nearly screamed from her end of the line, but managed to control herself enough not to.

"Hey. Rick. It's me."

"Sylvia. What can I do for you."

"I uhmm… I just wanted to know how you are doing," she said, untruthfully, as she began to lose her courage.

"I'm just fine. How about you, Detective?" Richard asked as he tried to think of a way of asking her out. He figured that he would have to, but he had to do it in such a way that she would believe that he thought that she was now back together with Dylan.

"I'm…"

Sylvia paused. She did not have the courage now, but she chose to have balls, like a man and said, "Can we meet?"

It was loud and the sound through the phone pierced Richard's ears. He was curious as to why she wanted to see him, but not enough to care. At least she had saved him from having to ask her. She had just asked for a warrant for her own death, and Judge King was happy to sign it.

"Tonight. Five-fifty. In the tall tree forest, on the outskirt of New York," he said and hung up. Sylvia jumped for joy in her bed, so much that her breasts slapped her in the face. She had done it. She now had her chance to get what she ultimately wanted. Happiness with Richard. She did not even question why he had chosen the tall tree forest. She was too excited.

Richard, at his desk, grinned. He now had more or less all he needed. But this meant he had to move fast. He shut his MacBook, grabbed his coat and headed out. He needed to go to the local liquor store. To buy a 'gift' for Dylan.

He bought Dylan a bottle of fine brandy. The same brand that the two of them had enjoyed the night before. He then went with it to the hotel Dylan was staying in. He knocked on Dylan's door and put his friendly face on. He had to move. Fast. Like the lightning in the distance. Before his window of opportunity closed.

"Rick?"

"Dylan," he said, holding up the bottle.

"What's this?"

"Some brandy."

"For what?"

"Can I come in?"

"Oh, yes, yes, of course."

Dylan moved aside, letting Richard in, with his bottle. "I wanted to give you this."

"Why?"

"Think of it as a mark. To the end of our feud and the beginning of our friendship."

Dylan was flattered. He did like the idea, that he could actually call the world-famous novelist, Richard 'Castle' King, his friend. And he loved the brandy the night before. He also knew that it was worth more than he could afford.

"A toast?" Richard asked, as he raised the bottle.

"Oh, sure. Glasses are over there," he said, pointing to the table behind Richard and smiling broadly. He also began to jump a slight bit.

"You need take a piss?"

"Yeah. Let me just go drain my little one."

"Okay. I'll be right here."

Dylan went into the bathroom to empty his bladder. The second the door closed; Richard got to work. He opened the bottle and poured two glasses of the brandy. He then liaised Dylan's with the drugs that had been delivered that morning.

He listened to the sound of Dylan's urine falling into the toilet, and it lasted an absurdly long time. Long enough that Richard had time to glance the room for the gun. He couldn't see it, but he noticed that the wardrobe door was slightly ajar and through it he could see a small safe, built into the wardrobe. It was the kind to store valuables, like jewellery, money or in this case, his money was on a work gun.

Dylan came out of the bathroom and Richard put on his friendly face again. He handed Dylan the glass of drugged brandy and said, "So... to friendship."

"To friendship."

They cheered and drank the contents of their glasses.

Within two minutes, Dylan said that he was feeling funny and walked towards the bed. His walk was shaky, and Richard grinned, while Dylan's back was turned towards him.

Within seconds, Dylan said, "Richard? Wha...?"

And fell over, onto the bed, and was out like a light. Richard smiled and looked at his watch. It was now twelve-fifty-eight. Which meant that Richard had until six-fifty-eight the next morning to commit the crime and get everything back into place.

Richard went and put his finger under Dylan's nostrils, to make sure he was still breathing. He was. He wasn't dead, which meant everything was going according to plan.

Richard went over to the wardrobe and looked at the safe. It was the kind that you could constantly reprogram the access code to, which meant only Dylan knew the code. But Richard knew that he had a poor memory and he wrote down all his passwords, on his phone.

He took Dylan's phone from the nightstand and took Dylan's index finger, and laid it over the phone's fingerprint scanner. It opened, and Richard was in. He went into the notes application and the very first one that popped up read '*Safe code – 12009*'.

It all seemed too easy. Richard punched in the code and the safe opened to reveal Dylan's gun. A Smith and Wesson Sigma nine millimetre.

A fine piece, he thought to himself.

Richard took the gun and a bullet clip that was next to it. He loaded the gun and put the safety on, hid it in his coat, took the access card for Dylan's room and left. He now had all he needed. But he needed to work out the last few details. How was he going to dispose of the body? For instance. He did not have the finer details worked out, and he did not have much time left.

He drove around for a fairly long time, until he stopped at the local clothes store. They were having a sale on winter gear. Jackets, raincoats, etcetera, due to the sudden storm that was expected to last a few days. The thing that caught his eyes though, were leather gloves. Everyone who has ever considered committing a crime, and who had a brain larger than a drop of water knows that it is wisest to wear gloves. Preferably, thick fabric ones.

You leave no fingerprints or DNA at the scene; you get no gunshot residue on your hands. He bought the gloves and checked his watch. It was now ten minutes to five. He had forty minutes to get to the tall tree forest.

The storm died down a bit and Richard grinned. The conditions seemed perfect.

Time was ticking… and soon Sylvia would meet her end.

Chapter 13

Richard arrived at the tall tree forest at five-twenty-one. Sylvia was not there yet; she was stuck in some traffic. She knew that Richard was a very punctual man, and that he would likely leave if she was not there on time, so she turned on her siren, illegally, and raced through the streets to meet Richard.

Richard got out of his car and looked up. He hoped that God would be able to forgive him for what he was about to do. He put on the gloves he had bought, and checked Dylan's gun. Since no one was around, he drew the gun and fired, to make sure it was working. It shot and he smiled.

Seconds later, he heard the sound of a police siren approaching. He turned around, fearing that a cop had heard the gunshot, and saw Sylvia's car coming up the winding road. He grinned, and thought to himself, '*It's time.*'

Sylvia pulled up her car, turned the engine and the siren off, and stepped out. She was wearing three and a half inch heels, and a very appealing jacket, with the zipper down and the three upper buttons of her shirt open, so Richard could see the gorge between her breasts and the strap that connected the cups of her bra. She had dressed this way because she was expecting to leave the forest with Richard, and going back to her place, for some more great sex.

"A little underdressed for this cold, aren't you?"

"Nope. I don't feel cold, in the least."

Sylvia shut her door and walked towards Richard, who was

perching on the bonnet of his car.

"So... how have you been?"

"Just fine, Detective."

Richard got up, and walked to his left. He was getting ready to draw the gun, but first he needed to be in a place where once the bullet had left the barrel of the gun, it would not end up striking either of the cars.

"And you?"

"I'm... I'm not that fine. I... I miss you."

Richard stopped dead in his tracks. He was surprised to hear this. "Why?" he asked, and began to walk more.

"Castle, I... I think I've fallen in love with you."

He was now surprised, but he was not sure how he felt about it. Not long before, he would have been overjoyed to hear those words from her mouth, but now... they did not have that effect on him. He stood still for several seconds and noticed that those words did not affect him, he knew then, that beyond a doubt, he was over her, and about to do many men of the world a huge favour.

Sylvia noticed his silence and was puzzled. She expected him to be jumping for joy, but instead he was emotionless. She began to walk towards him. Richard looked up and noticed that now he had a line of fire, such that the bullet would not hit either of the cars. It meant that it was time.

Richard drew the gun and aimed at Sylvia. She stopped moving towards him and stood still.

"So... you think that you can just wreak havoc with a man's feelings, break his heart, shatter his dreams of happiness and not suffer any consequences?"

"Castle... I... I'm offering you all the happiness you want, right now," she said, shocked and now desperate for her life, and she held up her breasts as a gesture that she was offering herself to him. She looked into his eyes. And she could not believe what she was seeing.

That twinkle of light that had been in his eyes, since the day they met. Even before Richard had officially professed his love to her. The twinkle of light that made her feel so special. The twinkle that made her feel like she could do anything. The twinkle that made her feel like the ultimate woman. The twinkle that made her feel smarter than Marilyn Vos Savant. The twinkle that made her feel sexier that Megan Fox and Nikki Minaj combined... it was gone.

Now she stood in front of Richard, and felt like nothing. She no longer felt special. Now she was no smarter than the twenty-one-year-old first grader, she was no sexier than the lady at the corner shop, who was so fat and round that you could use her as a bowling ball. She was no longer the ultimate woman who could do anything. She was no more noticeable than the anorexia girl down the street who barley had any breasts or curves. She felt... like nothing.

"Richard... please. I..."

Richard inhaled hard and held his breath, aiming for her head. He was a good shot, as he had proved at the department's shooting range, and this was one shot she couldn't miss.

Sylvia tried to gather up the guts to just try and beg Richard to spare her life, but she could see the determination in his eyes and she knew that it would be pointless. She shed a tear that fell onto her toes, and inhaled hard, closing her eyes, and waiting to her the bang.

Richard looked at her and knew that she was ready for him to make his move. He raised his thumb, made sure that the safety was off, and pulled the trigger.

The impact did not seem as instantaneous as he had imagined it would, but after what seemed like three and a half hours, he saw her fall over and bleed through her head. He exhaled heavily and walked over to her lifeless body. He knelt and felt for a pulse in her neck, and there wasn't a pulse. She... was... dead.

He sat and thought to himself for a second. He had just become a killer. It was something he had never imagined happening, but it had just happened. He shed a tear, out of the guilt of the horrific act he had just committed, and it landed right between Sylvia's breasts. He hoped for a few seconds that it would be like a fairy-tale, and his one tear would bring her back, but of course, it could not.

He rose to his feet, he had to continue with the plan, as there was no turning back now. He checked his watch. It was now five-forty-three. He still had plenty of time, but he needed to use it wisely and carefully.

He searched Sylvia's body and found her car keys. He was trying to come up with a good plan to dispose of her body when he felt the rain get heavier. It gave him an idea. They were overlooking the waters of the Atlantic Ocean. A brilliant idea was brewing in his head, and he decided to go along with it.

He dragged Sylvia's body to her car and put it in the driver's seat. He then, sitting in the back seat, took the back of her head and put the exit hole of the bullet and put it on the bullet hole in the back of her head and lined them up. Once lined up, he pulled the trigger and fired a shot through her head and out the windshield.

Now it looked like there had been someone who shot her from outside her car, as she was driving. He then went and did, roughly the same thing, but now with the bullet hole in her face, and shot again, so that there was a bullet hole in the headrest and back seats.

Now the car was set up, as the crime scene, he took her body out and laid it beside the car. He walked around, trying to find the three bullets and the three bullet casings that he had fired and the one he test fired before Sylvia arrived. He found them all, and took them with him, but he decided to purposefully leave one lodged in the material of the back seat.

That bullet, the police would later be able to link back to Dylan's gun, which would be what ultimately pointed to him as the killer, later on. Now what he needed was to find a corner in the road that overlooked the ocean. So, he dragged Sylvia's body to some bushes, about thirty-eight yards away, and left her there. He left his phone in Sylvia's car, to make it look like he and Sylvia were both still at the same place, together, then he jumped into his car and drove off. It took him less than five minutes and he found the perfect place to stage the rest of the crime.

He returned to where Sylvia's car was and went to her body. He now needed just one more thing, then the car would be the perfect crime scene. And the second he had it, he would need to move fast. He needed blood. Sylvia's blood. And once it was in the car, he would need to move fast, so that it would not dry up.

He took her lifeless body and dragged it back towards the car. He knew that he had to move fast, and get all of this over and done with. He took her head and bashed it against the seat headrest and steering wheel, so that the police would be certain of who was dead. Now he needed to be quick, if the blood dried up before he made it to the bend, it would look suspicious, as he wanted to make the police believe that she had been shot while driving, lost control of the car and gone over the road railing, and into the ocean in a matter of seconds.

He dragged her body back to the bushes, ran to the car and drove off, being careful not to put his head against the blood on the headrest or steering wheel, since it would create inconsistencies with his story. Now his car and Sylvia's body were still at the original scene, but he already had the perfect story to explain it all away.

Richard came to the straight stretch of road, which overlooked the bend and the ocean. He then had one last detail to add to the scene to try and throw himself further off the suspect list. He got out of the car and went to the front of the car, took the gun and aimed for the approximate area of where the front seat passenger's shoulder would be and fired a shot. He then went to the passenger seat, sat in it, put the gun to his shoulder, and shot himself.

The pain was beyond excruciating. Now he had a bullet wound to the upper left shoulder and was bleeding. He managed to put up with the pain and went to the back seat. Now there was another bullet lodged in the back seat, which was perfect. He took the bullet and casing of the first shot and put them in his pocket with the others.

Now, with Sylvia's blood on the steering wheel and driver's seat headrest, Richard's blood on the passenger seat, the two bullet holes in the windshield and the two bullets lodged in the back seats, Sylvia's car was the ultimate staged crime scene.

Richard noticed an abnormally large size stone on the side of the road, picked it up with his one hand and went back to the passenger seat of Sylvia's car. He took three deep breaths and then threw the huge, heavy stone onto the accelerator and the car took off heading for the bend that overlooked the Atlantic Ocean. The car was soon doing over one hundred miles an hour and Richard got ready for the impact.

The car struck the barrier and went through it. Now he was in the air, eighty metres above the water. As the car struck the barrier, Richard hit his head and he lost consciousness for a few seconds, until he could feel the ice-cold water on his skin, which revived him. The car resurfaced and Richard knew it would sink very quickly. He did not have much time now. He took the radio mic in the car and called in to the NYPD.

"This is Detective Castle, to all units! Detective Beckette and I are under attack! We have both been shot, and we've overshot the embankme…" His head dunked under the water, interrupting him.

"Embankment on the outskirts of th…" Again, his head dunked under the water, and interrupted him.

"The city! WE NEED HELP!" he said, with a few interruptions as he sank into the water, with the car.

Captain Johnson heard Richard's cries, through the communication channel.

"All units! Move to Detective Beckette and Richard's location! Right now! Repeat, all units are to help Detective Beckette and Richard, immediately! Right now! MOVE!"

Instantly, every air, land and sea unit in New York got to their transportation vehicles, turned on their sirens and raced to the location that Sylvia's car's Global Positioning Satellite pointed to. Johnson sprung up from his seat and ran to the helipad, to go with one of helicopters to the location, hoping that they were not too late.

Once Richard was done calling the police, he kicked open his door and escaped the car, as it sank to the bottom of the ocean. He swam, with his one functioning arm, to the surface of the water. He knew that the police wouldn't take long to arrive, but nonetheless, was shocked when he saw flashing lights in the sky, which were approaching, and he could hear sirens. It was faster than he had expected, so fast that he had no time to get his 'game face' on.

Richard, looking to the sky, suddenly realised a weight on the back of his hips. The gun.

Once the police arrived, he would need to be extra careful, so that they would not find the gun on him.

In less than two minutes, from when Richard escaped the car, there was a helicopter above him. An officer rappelled down from the helicopter to Richard. He hooked him to the rope and the two officers in the chopper pulled him up. Once Richard was aboard, he fell to the deck and coughed up some water. As he looked up, he realised that Benjamin, the Captain, was on board.

"Rick! Oh, thank God, you are all right! Where is Sylvia?"

"I… I don't know. She was in the car, when I last saw her," he said, untruthfully, as he stood, shivering, and holding the wound on his shoulder.

"What happened?"

"We were attacked."

"Are you hurt?"

Richard moved his hand, and showed him the bullet wound, still bleeding.

"He is wounded! He needs first aid."

"I'll be fine."

"Don't worry, we have the kit here."

Benjamin and Anthony took the first aid kit and began to treat Richard's shoulder. The officer who saved Richard from the water and Peter put on scuba gear and dived, to try and find Sylvia. Richard was having mixed feelings. It felt good that everything seemed to be going according to plan, but it was a bad plan for it to be going well. It was hard to feel good about murder.

As more and more units arrived on the water surface, on the road and in the air, a pair of helicopters dropped heavy prerecord ropes into the water, and three minutes later, pulled Sylvia's wrecked car from the water. Richard looked at it and then down at the water, where Peter and the other officer rose from the water and rappelled back up to the helicopter.

"And?"

"Where is she?", Richard and Ben asked them.

"There's no sign of her. The passenger side door was broken off, so… we assume her body was washed out by the water."

"I'm the one who broke open the door. Right after I called you guys in. The car was sinking and I had to escape."

"We understand, Rick."

Captain Johnson exhaled, hard, and picked up his mic.

"All water units, search the water for Detective Beckette. All other units, assist. Air unit nine, return to the station with the car. I want the forensics' team back at the station to start analysis on the car, ASAP."

He looked down at the water and told the pilot to take them back to the station. Richard had been treated, and now had a sling, supporting his shoulder and elbow. When they arrived at the station, Richard was cold, and acted shocked. Mr Johnson gave him some earl grey tea to warm him up.

The Captain, Anthony, the officer and Richard, sat in the empty police station, in silence.

"Richard, I know this has been traumatic for you, but unfortunately, we have to ask you. What exactly happened?"

Richard sat still, and said nothing, still pretending to be traumatised, and still thinking about the gun, which he was still carrying on his waist line, and still thinking about the time. He still had to put the gun back before six-fifty-eight, if he was even going to stand a chance of getting away with this.

The time now was twelve-twenty-four. Six hours and thirty-four minutes were left.

"It's okay, we can come talk to you tomorrow, when you have calmed down a bit," Ben said, and stood up.

"No. I... I'll tell you now. I mean... best do it now, while I still remember it best, right?"

"Thank you, Mr King."

Richard figured that he still had plenty of time, so why not get this done with, so that the only things to worry about, would be the gun and then Sylvia's body.

"We... we were... we were meeting up to discuss a future for us. We had... we had slept together and... and we... we were in love. She had asked me to meet with her so that we could talk about what she said to Dylan, the other night. That it was a mistake. And that... she wanted a future with me. I also wanted to tell her that I loved her and... and it went well. So, we decided to go out and have dinner out of town. Just the two of us. So, we got into her car and drove away. Then as we came around a bend and onto the road that overlooks the water, I heard a very loud bang. I ducked, in fear, and when I looked over to Sylvia, I... I saw... I saw her, with her... her head up against the steering wheel, and... and... and blood... on it.

"I leaned over to check if she was alive, but then... I heard another bang, and felt... the bullet go through my shoulder. And if I hadn't been leaning over to Sylvia, it might have got my heart. The pain of the wound was so excruciating, so I had to hold it. And as I did, I closed my eyes.

"The next thing was when I felt the car strike the barrier, and hit my head against the roof, as we went over the embankment and plummeted towards the water. When we landed in the water, the car began to sink and then I called in to the station with her radio mic. When I was done calling in to you guys, the car sank more and more. I had to find a way out, so I kicked down the door on my side and swam, with my one working arm to the surface, where you found me."

Richard began to cry, out of purpose of show, for them. They comforted him and eventually Benjamin offered to take him home. By this time a half hour had passed, and Richard did not want to go straight home. He first wanted to drop off the gun, but Mr Johnson wouldn't take no for an answer, and personally escorted Richard home.

When they arrived, Yvonne and Nathalie were worried sick, as they had seen the news, which showcased the story of Richard and Sylvia falling into the ocean.

"Oh, my son, are you okay?"

"Are you all right, Dad?"

"Oh, what happened?"

"I'm okay, guys, I'm fine."

They helped Richard to the couch and sat him down, where he still had to look shocked as Benjamin was still there.

"He will be fine. Fortunately for him, the bullet did not hit any vital organs, so he will be fine."

"What about Sylvia, Captain?"

"We... we haven't found her yet, Ms King."

"Oh, good Lord."

Captain Johnson, Yvonne and Nathalie sat with Richard, trying to make him feel better. Richard pretended to still be shaken up by what had happened, and kept checking the time. When his clock struck two o'clock, he decided to try and get Benjamin to leave and to create an opportunity for himself to go and return the gun.

Time was now against him. He had no car and he was now five miles away from the hotel where Dylan lay unconscious. Also, with his bullet wound and having to wear the sling to hold his arm, and he couldn't take a taxi to the hotel, because if the police ever found out, they would know, instantly, who it was, and it would be suspicious for him to be going to the hotel instead of resting. He had no choice, he would have to walk, and the sooner he left, the better. So, Yvonne and Nathalie had to go to bed and the Captain had to leave.

"I-I-I think I need to get some rest, guys."

"Oh, yes, of course. Try and relax, Richard."

"Thank you, Captain."

"I'll come and check on you in the morning, and fill you in on what happens."

Benjamin left, and Richard went to his room, fell on his bed and pretended to be asleep. Yvonne and Nathalie on the other hand, remained awake. They were shocked. They believed that they had nearly lost the most important man in their lives, and it really hit them hard.

Yvonne had a few glasses of wine, and Nathalie went to the kitchen, to bake some muffins for her father, as a gift for him, in the morning.

Richard lay on his bed, looking at his digital clock, beside his bed. Time was moving, and the two ladies needed to go to bed soon, or he would never make it in time.

When he finally heard Nathalie and Yvonne say goodnight to each other, and saw the lights go out, he sprung up from his bed. It was now four-forty-seven. He now had two hours and eleven minutes, to travel five miles, on foot. And then even less time to return before Yvonne and Nathalie woke up.

He got up from the bed, with his one working arm, quietly,

snuck out of his room and to the doorway of his mother's. As he did, he saw her alarm clock, set for eight o'clock. That was now the time he had to be back by. He got his shades from his office, his coat from the coat hanger and left.

He didn't have time on his side, so he had to speed walk, but the pain of the bullet wound slowed him down. He finally arrived at the hotel, an hour and fifty minutes after he left. Now, he needed to get in, without being seen. Once again, the broken arm would have been a complete giveaway, if anyone saw it and told the police about it, even if it only happened decades later. He now had twenty-one minutes, so he had to be quick.

He went around to the back, but found that the employee-only entrance was locked. Richard had no choice, he had to use the front door. He took three deep breaths, pulled the side of his coat, so that it would cover his sling as best possible, and went right through the front entrance. He exhaled in relief to find that there was no one at the reception desk. However, he mistakenly looked up and noticed a surveillance camera. Now it had caught his face. That was not good.

He walked up to the elevator shaft, and found that it was out of order, it seemed that someone had broken it that day. So, the stairs it was, then. He climbed three flights of stairs and suddenly, the pain from his wound got much worse. He stopped and nearly cried, but checking his watch, and seeing that he had seven minutes left, he knew he had to push, as if he were about to give birth, and get the job done.

He finally made it to the floor that Dylan was staying on, with three minutes left. He scanned the key card, let himself in and found Dylan laying exactly where Richard had left him. Richard opened the safe, put the gun back in the safe, left the key card where he had found it and got ready to walk out, when he realised the glass that Dylan had drank from. Even though it had no taste or anything, if that glass was ever checked for evidence, it would show the drugs that Richard had used on Dylan.

So, he took the glass, emptied the last few drops of brandy that were in it, into the bathroom toilet and tossed the glass out the window. As he went to the door and looked back, he saw Dylan's arm move and heard a very faint groan from him. It was now six-fifty-eight and the drug had worn off. Richard scoffed to himself, gently shut the door behind him and walked down the passageway.

Dylan awoke and felt very numb. He struggled to move his limbs, but he was now awake and looking around. Everything seemed perfectly in order. His assumption was that the brandy that Richard had bought for him was much stronger than he expected, and glanced at the bottle on the counter. He tried to get up, but couldn't, so he closed his eyes and went back to sleep.

Richard had done it. Well, most of it. He still had a few last things to do. He needed to get home in time, he needed to erase the surveillance feed from the cameras in the hotel for that day, and he needed to dispose of Sylvia's body. But one thing at a time. Now, he needed to get home, in one hour and two minutes. Which meant he had to run, as fast as his tired and murderous legs could carry him.

He was a bit less than half a mile away from home when he checked his watch for the seven thousandth time that morning, and it struck seven- forty-one. Nineteen minutes left. He couldn't believe it. He was terribly out of breath, in a lot of pain and very tired, but it looked like he would make it.

He ran as fast as he could in his state and got to the building at seven-fifty- four. He had six minutes left and was feeling relieved, until he realised the cameras of the building. They would see him, if he used the main door, and he already had enough to worry about. The cameras at the building would already need to be erased from the previous night as well, as they would show him leaving the penthouse. To save himself the effort of having more footage to erase later, he chose to go in through the underground parking entrance.

He ducked under the pillar that raised and lowered to allow cars in, went in, and headed straight for the elevator. Suddenly he heard the roar of an engine. One that sounded familiar. He turned his head and saw his car, being followed by Mr Johnson's car.

He panicked and ducked behind the nearest parked car. Many, many thoughts went through his mind as he hid behind the car. If they had gone to his car, did they find Sylvia's body? After all, he had left it so close to his car. He peeked round the corner of the car he was hiding behind and saw his car come to a complete stop. Mr Johnson stepped out and Anthony and Peter came out from Mr Johnson's car. If they were here, it was to see him. He needed to get upstairs, to the penthouse. And he had just under three minutes to do so.

With them now there, he was never going to make it to the elevator before them, unless they got distracted. He noticed a piece of gravel beside his foot. He had only one idea, it was crazy and stupid, but it was so crazy and stupid that it might just work. He picked it up, with his functioning arm, peeked round the corner and tossed it towards a van that was parked a few spaces away from him.

It shattered the windshield and set off the alarm. The three policemen, in their instincts ran to the van, with the alarm blaring. Richard crept round the corners of the car he was hiding behind and made a quiet run for the elevator. His watch showed that he had one minute and twenty- six seconds left.

The elevator arrived at the penthouse floor, and Richard ran to the penthouse door. He opened and shut it quietly, put his coat on the coat hanger, went to his office to put down his shades, and went to his room. As he passed his mother's room, he looked at her digital clock, where the digital second counter showed that it was five seconds before eight o'clock. He went to his room, took off his shoes and took cover under the blanket, just as he heard her alarm go off.

Yvonne and Nathalie woke up, upon hearing the alarm and went to Richard's room, to check on him. As they looked at him, he lay on the bed, pretending to be asleep. However, what did frighten them was the fast-paced breathing that Richard was doing. It was from his exhaustion of running from the hotel back home, and he could not hide it. Thinking that Richard was suffering a heart attack or something of the sort, Yvonne ran to him, crying,

"Richard! Richard!"

"Aaaaaaahhhhhhhhhh!"

Richard screamed and jumped out from the blankets, pretending to be frightened.

"Are you okay, son?"

Richard continued to breathe hard, from his exhaustion, and claimed that he had been having a nightmare, and his mother's cries had frightened him more some.

The three of them then heard the doorbell ring. Richard knew, it was the captain and the two detectives. Yvonne and Nathalie didn't but went to open the door, to discover that it was them anyway.

As the two ladies left Richard alone in the bedroom, he breathed a sigh of relief. He had done it. He was almost done with everything. All that was left was to wipe the footage of himself from his building, the hotel, and he needed to get rid of Sylvia's body. The second he thought of that, he remembered that the three men had brought back his car. That meant that they had been extremely close to where he had hidden her body. That was worrying. If they had found it, he was now a dead man walking.

"Richard, Benjamin and his two detectives are here to see you!"

"Coming, Mother."

Well, now it was time to see exactly what they had found out. Richard put his game face on, the face of the wounded victim, and went to the living room, to speak to the three men.

It was nerve wrecking, not knowing what they knew, but it had to be done. It was now do or die time for Richard 'Castle' King.

Chapter 14

He got up from the bed and went to the living room, to see the three men.

"Gentlemen."

"Rick. How are you holding up?"

"About as good as can be expected," he said to them, rubbing his eyes.

"That's good. Well, we are here to check on you and update you on our findings."

"Okay."

"Oh, we also brought your car back for you."

"Oh. Thank you, gentlemen. So, did you find anything?"

Yvonne and Nathalie came and sat down with the four men in the living room. They too were eager to hear what they had found. Richard was very nervous to hear if they had or hadn't found her body yet.

"There has been no sign of Detective Beckette's body yet. The scuba teams and water units searched all night, but it seems her body was washed away, with the current of the water."

Yvonne, Nathalie and Richard hung their heads in disappointment of the bad news that had befallen their ears. Richard was relieved, but he couldn't show it, he had to hide it from the three authority men, but he was greatly relieved.

"However, we do have some good-ish news," Peter added on. Richard nearly flinched, as pretty much any good news for them would be bad news for him. He had to maintain his composure, just a bit longer. Anthony finished up the story for them.

"In the car, we found traces of human blood, on the seats and on the steering wheel. Even though it was washed off by the water, we had enough for DNA comparisons. Before we came here, we received confirmation that the blood on the passenger seat is indeed yours, Mr King. The other sample confirms all that you said. It is indeed that of Sylvia Beckette."

Peter took over and continued what Anthony was saying.

"And based on the position of the blood and the bullet hole, in does indeed indicate that Sylvia would have been shot in the head and, based on what you said, that you were leaning over to Sylvia's body when you were shot, the evidence is consistent with the location of your gunshot wound."

So, in all honesty, this was good news for Richard. All was going according to his plan. The scene was staged perfectly.

"Yeah. And we also found the two bullets. Lodged in the back seats. So, given that, we can indeed confirm that Sylvia could not have survived the bullet. Since it went through her head, it would have penetrated her brain and killed her instantly," Mr Johnson said to the family of three.

To Yvonne and Nathalie, none of this was good news, but to Richard, it was exactly what he wanted to hear. He had staged everything perfectly. This meant that the chances of him being caught were slim to none. Finally, Anthony finished up the report.

"Also, the bullets we found in the back seats, they have, what we in the business refer to as Lands and Grooves. Mr King, I'm sure you know what that means. It means we have the 'fingerprint' of the weapon that shot you and killed Sylvia. We are currently running the markings through the FBI database. So, if it a registered gun, we'll find it very soon."

The King family sat still in silence. Yvonne and Nathalie in shock, and Richard out of the act he had to put on. He was glad with their findings but hid it from them very well.

"Thank you, guys."

"You're welcome, Mr King. Anyway, we have to get back to the crime scene now. We'll fill you in if we get any more information."

"Thank you."

Richard saw them out of the penthouse and went to his room. Believing that he was tired and shocked, Yvonne and Nathalie let him go, and did not disturb him. Instead, they showered and went out for breakfast, leaving Richard alone.

Richard heard them leave and wandered the house, thinking to himself. He did not know how to feel. He was now a killer, and that was nothing to be proud of. But he seemed to be getting away with it. That was a good thing. Wasn't it?

He went to his desk and thought to himself for a while. He now needed a plan. He had a few last loose ends to clean up, and he needed to do it fast.

He couldn't think. He was too tired, so he went to sleep. He awoke six hours later, at three-twenty-eight. The ladies were back, and he was feeling better. He was now smelling from his armpits and his scrotum, and went for a nice cold shower. It refreshed him and he was now feeling as right as the heavy rains falling outside. Well, besides his bullet wound.

After a cup of coffee and a warm meal, he felt as good as you can after murdering someone. Now he needed to do the finishing touches on the crime. First the cameras in the building. He already had the perfect idea.

He took his phone and went downstairs to the woman at the

reception desk of the building. He spoke to her and flirted with her while scanning the frequency from the main computer with his phone. Once he had scanned it, he cloned it and went back up to the penthouse, without her even realising what he had done.

He went back up to the penthouse, to his office and sat at his desk. He used the frequency of the reception computer to hack into the system of the building and erased all the footage on the cameras, from when he left to go and put back Dylan's gun, up to when he returned that morning. Now, all that was left was the body and the footage at the hotel.

Richard had an idea, but he was not so sure about some of the finer details. And he needed a few things. He needed Dylan's ID card and driver's license. But how to get hold of them was another story. By now, it was nearly six o'clock in the evening. He was feeling much better than that morning, and the bullet wound was not too painful. He was about to join his mother and daughter in the kitchen, when the doorbell rang. He answered it, and found it was Anthony, Peter and Benjamin.

"Two visits in one day, gentlemen?"

"Hello Richard. May we come in?"

"Oh, yes, of course."

"Thank you."

Yvonne and Nathalie were very interested in what they had to say. "Would you like to join us for dinner, gentlemen?"

"Uhmm, no, thank you, Ms King. We aren't going to be very long."

"Okay..."

Benjamin took a deep breath and heavily let it out.

"Mr King, we told you we would come and see you if anything came up, and well... something has come up."

Richard almost flinched, he was frightened by the Captain's

serious tone. Had they found something in the car that pointed to him as the killer? After all, if it was something less sinister, they would have just phoned him to tell him.

"The bullets that I told you we found... we found a registered gun than matched the Lands and Grooves on the bullets to a T."

Yvonne, Nathalie and Richard looked at them, with a hard stare. "It's the gun provided and registered to FBI Agent Dylan Anderson."

Richard was very relieved that they had now got Dylan as the prime suspect, but Yvonne and Nathalie were quite confused.

"Who?"

"Dylan Anderson. He's an old friend that Sylvia and I met at high school. He was also assigned to help us with the last case we worked on. The one about the doctors."

Nathalie gasped in horror. She had never met or seen Dylan, yet both ladies were shocked by what Richard had just told them. That the man who shot him and killed Sylvia was one of their friends. One who had sworn and oath to protect citizens of America, and instead had taken the life of a well-respected NYPD detective, and nearly killed the man that they loved most.

"He's staying in a hotel not far from here. We are on our way to pick him up now."

"Good!"

"Richard? Would you like to come with us?"

Richard put on a mask, one that made him appear angry and upset. Behind it, he was smiling. Everything was going exactly the way it was supposed to. And he had an idea. If they were going to 'pick' Dylan up at the hotel, he would have a chance to get the frequency of the hotel's computerised network, so that he could erase the footage, and he could get Dylan's ID card and

Driver's license.

"Yeah. Yeah, I'll come with you."

Richard said, in a disguised voice that made him sound angry. He grabbed his coat, and went downstairs with them. The four men drove off, through the heavy storm and went to the hotel to speak to Dylan, who was not expecting anything.

When they arrived, Anthony made it clear that they did not have a warrant for Dylan's arrest, which meant that they could only take him in, if he agreed. Richard pretended to be distraught, but he did not care deep down. He was only there for three small things, and he was going to get them.

As the four men walked through the lobby, to the reception desk. Since the three other men did not know what room Dylan was in, they had to ask the receptionist. Richard took his broken arm and pulled his phone out of his shirt pocket. He did exactly what he had done at the building he stayed in. He cloned the frequency of the reception computer, and he would use it to erase the footage of the previous night, that showed him at the hotel. He was careful and hid his face from the receptionist, so that she would not point out that he already knew which room Dylan was staying in.

Once she had told the four of them, they went up the stairs, since the elevator was broken, to Dylan's room. Captain Johnson knocked on the door, and Dylan opened it.

"Oh. Gentlemen. How can I help you?"

"May we come in, Agent Anderson?"

"Of course."

As they walked in, Dylan noticed that Richard was wearing an arm support. He was quite surprised and as such, he asked,

"What happened to your arm, Rick?"

Richard kept quiet and closed his eyes, pretending that he

thought Dylan was pretending. Anthony answered Dylan's question.

"He was shot."

"Shot? Wha… When?"

"Last night."

Dylan looked at them, genuinely surprised and fairly confused. He did not understand. And he was now even more puzzled by their visit.

"Where is your gun, Agent Anderson?"

"My gun?"

"Yes."

"It… It's in the safe. Why?"

"Please give it to me."

"Uhmm… sure."

Dylan walked over to the safe, and as he did, Richard caught sight of Dylan's wallet, on the nightstand, beside the bed. While everyone was facing the other way, Richard walked over to it and put it in his coat.

As Dylan opened the safe and took out his gun, Anthony asked him to put it in his evidence bag. Dylan was now even more confused. Richard asked to use Dylan's bathroom, and he obliged.

Richard went into the bathroom and immediately opened the wallet. He found what he was looking for right in front. Dylan's US ID card and driver's licence. He took them and put them in his trousers pocket.

Outside, he could overhear Peter telling Dylan that Sylvia was dead, and that bullets in the car pointed to his gun as the murder weapon. Dylan was now majorly confused and since he truly was innocent, he denied being involved in the shooting. Richard took some water in a cup and poured it down the toilet, to make it sound like he was urinating. He stepped out of the bathroom, and found Dylan in a frenzy. He had to try very hard not to smile as he went and sat on Dylan's bed.

Dylan continued to deny that he had done anything and the three NYPD officers asked Dylan to come down to the station with them. He truly had nothing to hide and so willingly obliged. For a few seconds, the four of them looked away, and Richard used those seconds to put Dylan's wallet back on the nightstand, while Dylan got his coat, and the other three headed for the exit.

The five of them left and went outside to the car in the rain. Richard had gotten all he needed and so told Captain Johnson that he did not want to go to the station with them, and to drop him back at home. They all understood what Richard was feeling and did as he wished. They left him in the underground parking lot of his building. As the four of them drove off, Richard smiled and almost laughed, with maniacal delight.

He turned out to be a good criminal. But it also seemed very wrong, as he was admonishing a man for his own sins. However, it had to be done.

Richard went upstairs, in silence, walked right past the two ladies and went straight to his office. Presuming that he was upset by what was happening, they left him be watched television in the living room.

Richard plugged his phone into his laptop and began the process of erasing the footage of the previous night, at the hotel. It did not take him very long, and he succeeded. He now had only one thing left to worry about. The body. He knew that by now rigor mortis would have set in, and he knew that he had get the body moved as quickly as possible, before it started to decompose. Since it had been raining ever since her death, the decomposition process would not have begun, but he had to move fast. Soon this would all be behind him, and he would be free.

He went to the living room and watched Family Feud with his family, until they decided to go to sleep. Before he went to sleep, he decided to put the last part of his plan in motion, and called Captain Johnson.

"Hello?"

"Hi, Ben. It's me. Richard King."

"Ahh. Mr King. How are you doing?"

"I'm fine. Look I just wanted to know how it went with… *him.*"

"Well, he denied everything, and since we didn't have a warrant, we couldn't place him under arrest."

"Oh…"

"I'm sorry, Mr King, but we should have a warrant soon."

"It's okay. Thanks."

"You take care of yourself now."

"Yeah. I will."

Richard experienced mixed emotions after that conversation. He was glad that Dylan was still free, because it gave him an opportunity to go and dispose of the body. However, it also meant that there was not enough to throw Dylan in prison, so the investigation would continue, giving the police a chance to maybe find something that pointed to him as the killer.

By this time, it was nearly half past nine, and Richard needed to get the last part of the job done. And fast. He went to sleep, and set his alarm for three-thirty the next morning. He woke up when the alarm went off, and fortunately did not wake up Yvonne and Nathalie. He did his morning ablutions, emptied his bladder, showered etcetera and got dressed.

The weather was still pouring rain on the city of New York,

and the conditions were perfect for the last part of his grand crime. He went to the kitchen and took a strong pain killer, and then removed the brace from around his arm and shoulder. It still hurt, but not too badly. He stretched it out and the joints cracked from stiffness. It hurt, but it needed to be done if he was going to pull off this last bit.

He wrote a note to his mother and Nathalie, saying '*Morning guys. I had to go out to meet my publisher, for the book. We need to discuss a few things and start arranging the cover art. I'll probably be gone a while. You can order some breakfast, since it is my turn to prepare breakfast. Love you both. XXX.*'

He left a hundred bucks with the note on the kitchen counter and went out, with his umbrella, coat, dark shades, a pair of leather gloves and a lot of cash. He had an eight-and-a-half-mile walk to start. To a local car rental place. More specifically a place to rent out vans. That was what he needed Dylan's ID and Driver's licence for. So that he could rent the van out under Dylan's name. This was also why he needed Dylan to be out of prison, because if the documents he was going to fill out as Dylan ever got to the police, it wouldn't make sense if 'Dylan' rented out the van, while he was in prison. He had also brought along a lot of cash for this, so that no one would be able to trace his credit card.

Richard arrived at the van rental shop around six-forty-one. They had only been open for eleven minutes, by then. Richard went inside and spoke to the man at the reception desk.

"Hello."

"Hello sir. What can we help you with today?"

"I need a van. As in right now."

"Of course, sir. Uhmm... for how long do you need it?"

"Twenty-four hours."

"All right then. Here. Just fill in these two forms. Oh, and I'll need to see your driver's licence and ID card."

"Of course. Here."

Richard handed him Dylan's ID and licence. He had printed out a pair of pictures of himself at home, and overlaid them on Dylan's pictures on the ID card and licence.

"Sir, could you please take your glasses off?"

"Oh, yeah, sure thing."

Richard removed his glasses and revealed his face to the man. The man was satisfied and had confirmation of the man's identity. He now believed that Richard was Dylan Anderson. Richard finished off the paperwork and handed it over to the man.

"Okay, this looks good. Let me go get you the keys."

"All right."

Richard gave a sigh of relief. He could not believe that he had actually pulled it off. As he looked up however, he caught sight of a camera.

Now there was one more thing to add to his to do list. He had to erase the footage from this camera system too. So, he did exactly as he had done at his building and the hotel. He took out his phone and began cloning the frequency of the reception computer, to create a backdoor into the system, which he would access later.

"All right, Mr Anderson. That will be one thousand, six hundred dollars."

"Of course."

Richard pulled out his wallet and counted out sixteen hundred-dollar notes. He handed them to the man, who was slightly puzzled. A modern man of New York, using cash, instead of a credit card. That was bizarre.

"Cash, sir?"

"Yes. Problem?"

"No, no, no... it's just a bit... unusual."

"Well... here."

"Thank you, sir."

The man took a second and began counting the money. The total was correct, and he said to Richard,

"Okay, Sir. It's the van parked in parking bay one-C. You have until seven-twenty-seven to get the van back here tomorrow. A second longer, and there will be a thousand-dollar penalty."

"A thousand dollars?"

"Yes, Sir. Its standard policy."

"Well, okay then. Have a good one."

"You too, Mr Anderson."

Richard walked outside to the parking bays, and got the van in bay one-C. He quickly slid under the van, and disabled the Global Positioning Satellite chip, then entered the car. He exhaled, in relief and drove off. Now, it was time for the most pain staking clean up job. Disposing of Sylvia's body.

He drove and reached the location where he and Sylvia had met two days earlier. As he pulled up, he began to feel queasy. He was about to handle a dead body, and for the first time ever, he actually thought of it as stomach turning. None the less though, it had to be done.

He exited the van, put on some leather gloves that he had brought with him and walked over to where he had left Sylvia's body. As he walked over to it, he noticed that the rain was starting lighten up a bit, which was a good and a bad thing for him.

He walked into the bush he had hidden Sylvia's body in and found her still lying there. There was water dripping from her face, and insects beginning to crawl over her corpse, but fortunately for him, she had not begun to decompose. He looked at her, and for a few seconds felt guilty about what he had done to her and what he was about to do. He went and picked up her shoulders and began to carry her towards the back of the van. She was heavy now, and his injured shoulder hampered his strength, but he thought he could do it.

After about two minutes, he had not gone very far, and he heard a tearing sound. The sound of a material tearing. He checked his clothes and they were just fine. He then realised that it was Sylvia's clothes he could hear tearing, as they were getting caught in the vegetation.

Richard knew that he couldn't continue to move her like this, because if any scraps of Sylvia's clothes were found here; it would contradict his story that he had given to the police.

He knew what he had to do, and so, he began the painstaking task of undressing Sylvia's corpse. It felt very strange. For the eight years before, it was his dream to undress her, but now… it was nothing short of nerve wrecking.

Once he had undressed Sylvia's corpse entirely, he went back to the van and threw her clothes into the back. He then dragged her naked body to the van and loaded it in the back. He did not have to worry about anybody showing up and asking questions because of the harsh weather that had struck New York. He shut the backdoors of the van, got behind the wheel, and drove off.

He passed a small town on the way, as he drove, and decided to stop. He needed a few things now. A saw, some gasoline, and a cigarette lighter. He drove a few miles more, and then stopped the car. He left the car hidden in some bushes and walked back to the town to get what he needed.

Upon his return, about an hour later, he got to the van with all he needed. A fairly long saw, a jerry can, filled with gasoline, and a cigarette lighter. He found the van exactly as he had left it, and it did not seem as though anyone had seen what was in the back.

He then drove off, a fair distance until he came up to a forest. By this time, he was over three hours away from New York City, and this seemed like the perfect place to carry out the last of his plan. He parked the van in the middle of the forest, shut off the engine and went to the back.

He opened the back doors and took the saw he had bought and went to work. He sawed off as many branches from nearby trees as he could, and then laid them out near the back of the van. He then began the painstaking task of dragging Sylvia's naked body out of the van, and to the wood he had cut and laid out eight feet away.

As he did so, with his broken arm, it gave way, and he felt the excruciating pain from his self-inflicted bullet wound. He knelt and fell to the ground in pain, and then looked back to the body. He was so close to pulling off the perfect murder and getting away with it. He was not going to let the pain stop him from succeeding.

He ignored the pain and continued to drag Sylvia's corpse over to the wood he had cut, and laid her over it. He breathed, heavily, from the exhaustion and pain that he went through, but now everything was ready. He returned to the van and got the jerry can, which he had filled with gasoline and walked back towards the body.

He opened it, and sprinkled the gasoline all over Sylvia's dead, naked body. He was very emotional about it. He could not believe what he was about to do the woman he had once loved. He poured and poured the gasoline on and around her, until the can was empty. He put the can back in the van and then went back to the body.

He stared down at her body and his emotions began to take over. This was the woman he wanted to say 'I do' to. What was he doing? What had he done? He had had let his anger get the better of him. His emotions had gotten ahead of him, and clouded his judgement. But now, he was neck deep in the crime, and so he had to finish it.

As some of the clouds above him parted, the moonlight shone through, for a few seconds, and reflected in a single drop of the gasoline, on Sylvia's body.

Richard caught sight of the drop, in the very corner of Sylvia's left eye, and next to her nose. He looked at it and the drop in her eye brought back a memory. It was from the earliest days when he first met her. He remembered how they got along and became good friends. He remembered a day where the two of them sat on the field, at school, and he first looked into her shining eyes. The light that they shone to his heart caused his blood to boil and rush through his veins. It felt like there was a fever burning him, deep inside.

He then came back to reality, and watched as the force of gravity and the wind that blew through his hair, pushed the gasoline drop away from her eye and around the left edge of her nose. The drop went past her cheek and to her upper lip, like a tear.

As the drop went around the left side of her mouth and headed for her chin, another memory was triggered. A memory of when he heard her voice sing to his heart, as they did their homework together one afternoon after school. The feeling of the notes from her angelic voice as they went through his ears and to his heart, was one that made him feel like, despite all the corruption and problems in the world, he was in heaven. Each time the words of her sweet voice touched his heart.

His attention came back to the drop that had been carried around her mouth and was now on her chin. The wind and natural forces pushed the drop off the edge of her chin and it fell to her chest. It continued and flowed between her exposed breasts, as they jiggled slightly. A third memory came to him.

The memory of the night that they had sex, less than a fortnight before. He was reminded of how perfect her body was that night, and how her breasts were the best he had ever seen. How she just had the perfect body, which in his eyes surpassed any other woman who had ever lived and died.

The drop recaptured his attention again, as it continued to flow across her torso and came to her belly button. Another memory came to Richard's mind. A memory again from high school. A memory of himself and Sylvia, as they played on the field one afternoon, after school, tickling each other.

Her laughter was such that it triggered his own. Her happiness, and her smile shone brighter than ten suns, combined. It filled him with happiness as he tickled her that afternoon, and as he stared at her smile and listened to her laughter, the world seemed to stand still. For that time, it felt like all in the world was in perfect balance and their hearts seemed to beat in perfect harmony.

Richard's vision suddenly became blurry, as a tear came up from his left eye. The single drop of gasoline, reached the end of her stomach and ran across her groin. It continued, and flowed across the centre of her vagina. Again, a memory played in his mind. A memory of the experience he had, being inside her as they had sex, and how she amazing it was to have sex with the woman that he loved.

The tear in his eye fell off the edge of his eyelid and flowed down his cheek, as he watched the drop of gasoline reach the tip of Sylvia's vagina. The corpse's legs were spread apart, the gasoline drop had reached the vulva, and fell off the tip of Sylvia's dead body hit the ground.

As the drop fell to the ground, and burst into droplets, one last memory played in Richard's mind. The memory of her standing in front of him, and himself as he pulled the trigger.

The recalling of the bang, as he pulled the trigger corresponded with the moment that the tear that was flowing along his face, reached his chin and fell onto Sylvia's body. Right onto the nipple of her left breast.

The memory of him taking her life frightened him, immensely. He jumped as his mind came back to reality and he took several steps back, from the corpse.

Was that who he was now? Because of her? A murderer?

He stood still and shook his head. No. He could not lose his guts and confidence now. He was so close to getting away with this. He had to go through with the last part of his masterpiece of a plan. He had to lock his emotions up, and be in control. One thing he had learnt from Sylvia was, let your brain control you. Not your heart.

He turned around, and faced the body once more. He closed his eyes, and looked down, as he drew the cigarette lighter he had bought from his coat pocket.

He lit it, locked the flame, and tossed it to the corpse, which was smothered in gasoline and had firewood beneath it. It seemed to stay in the air for ages before it landed on Sylvia's breast. Within seconds, the corpse was being incinerated, by the gigantic flame, as it consumed and hid the body behind a curtain of flames.

The wood beneath the corpse, added strength to the fire, and the gasoline, as an accelerant, made the flames bigger and hotter.

Richard watched from beside, as the flames grew and eventually completely hid Sylvia from him. The wind blew through his hair and coat, making them flutter in the wind, as he watched the corpse of the woman, he once loved burn, to a crisp.

He walked back to the van, and took her clothes, that he had removed from her corpse, out of it. He walked back to the blazing fire that was eating through Sylvia's flesh like termites through wood and began to throw them into the scorching flames, one by one.

He stood there for almost ten minutes and he had set most of her clothes ablaze. He was now at the last three items. He threw her shirt in as carelessly as the rest of her clothes, and now was down to the last two items. Ironically, they were the two most sexual clothing items she had worn the day that she died. Her bra and her panties.

He clenched the panties in his palm and got ready to throw it in like the other items, but he found that they triggered some thought. This was one of the panties that had hidden her vagina from the world. His thoughts turned to her what it is that she never got to do with her vagina. She had never brought a new life into the world with it. She had never been a mother to anyone. And he was the reason that she never did, because he took away her capability to have children, when he drew the gun, and killed her.

A tear came up in his eye, as he looked into his other hand, where he was holding her bra. A similar thought came to his mind. This was one of the bras that she had used to hold up her breasts and show them off to the world. He thought about how she had never got the chance to use hers the way that they were intended to be used. She had never breastfed a child with them. She never had the chance to be a mother. To nurture and raise a child, and it was him who took away her chance to.

He held one of the bra cups in each of his hands and rubbed the inside of the cups with his thumbs. Feeling how soft they were, and imagining how she felt, having her breasts and nipples against this material, he cried to himself. He was now beginning to grasp the number of things he had robbed the world of. A daughter, a sister, a niece, a potential mother, a policewoman. There was so much that he had robbed the world of because of his own, personal vendetta with her.

He didn't want to throw the panties and bra into the flames. He wanted them to remind him of her. How it was like to sleep with her. How he loved her. But he knew that he could not. If anyone ever found them, he would become and instant suspect. They had to go.

Richard clenched the thirty-two-inch waist panties and the thirty-eight- D bra and launched them into the air. Time, once again, seemed to pass slower than it did, but eventually the bra and panties disappeared into the flames. The fire grew bigger as they landed in it, and Richard fell to his knees and cried, as he watched the fire consume her flesh and clothing.

He knelt beside the flame a while and when the rain got heavier, he went to his van, trying to avoid catching a cold. He sat behind the steering wheel, lay his arms over the top of it and hung his head on his folded arms. He wept and wept for the woman her once loved and had robbed the world of, as he sat behind the wheel of the world.

"I really did love you, Sylvia," he cried to himself.

He wept for several minutes, until he remembered what it was she had done to him, and why he had taken her life. His reasons were valid, and he did not need to hide them. She deserved to die at his mercy for one simple reason, and she had.

The reason… was his heartbreak.

Chapter 15

Richard looked in his rear-view mirror, at the blazing fire behind him. He noticed that the flames were getting smaller. He then paid more attention to his ears. He could hear rain. Heavy rain, as it came down onto the car's windshield.

The rain was back, and quite strong. The fire had not completed the job yet. Richard took the umbrella out of the back and walked over to what was left of Sylvia's incinerated corpse. The fire had completely devoured all her clothes, all her flesh and all her body tissue, but it had not finished the job.

There were still several bones of hers that did not get destroyed before the rains came down. Her skull, her pelvis, her arms, her legs and part of her spine. They were already badly damaged from the fire, but he needed them to disappear too. It was just about a fifth of her body, and they needed to disappear too.

Richard did not have time to waste, waiting for the rain to stop and then burn them to powder like the rest of her bones had been. He needed to return the van on time and get home before his mother and daughter got suspicious. There was only one thing to do. Dispose of them manually.

Richard took Sylvia's burnt skull, and picked it up with his hands, which were still enclosed with his leather gloves. He put down the umbrella and used his now free hand to punch the jaw area of the skull. The reason being, that if anyone ever found this, they could not use dental records to confirm that this was her.

He then walked over to the van and began the nerve wrecking task of moving the last of Sylvia's bones into the back of the van. He loaded them in, one by one, apart from one of her arms and her skull. These he would dispose of right here.

He took a shovel from the back of the van, that he had found there, when he rented it out. He began to dig a pair of shallow pits, and left the skull in one, and the arm bone in the other.

He buried them and then got back in the van. He knew exactly what he was going to do with them. There was a route that followed the coast line from where he was back to New York. It was going to make the trip back to New York longer, but he did not have any other ideas.

Following the road to the road that overlooked the ocean did not take long, and now he was looking at the ocean water. He stopped, and took Sylvia's pelvic bone from the back of the van. He walked to the railing, on the road and threw the pelvic bone, with all his might, into the water, deep down below.

He heard the splash and gave a blunt grin to himself. This is how he would dispose of the bones. Tossing them into the water, at random points along the coastline. And so, he did. Stopping at random intervals, he threw Sylvia's remaining bones into the ocean, one by one.

Finally, he came to the last bone, and by now he was not far from the police search site, where police were still looking for her body. It was one of her leg bones. He threw it into the ocean and once he heard the splash, he knew that his job was done. He had now successfully disposed of Sylvia's body, and most of the evidence. He felt about as good as he possibly could in that moment, and drove off.

Now he only had a few things left to do. He had to reactivate the Global Positioning Satellite chip, return the van and delete the footage from the rental shop. These were all menial tasks, considering what he had already done.

He pulled over, once he re-entered New York, and got out. He reactivated the chip in the bonnet and then drove it back to the dealership that he had rented it from.

He parked the car in the bay he took it from and then went inside. He took all the things that he had brought with him, and that he had bought, apart from the jerry can and the saw, which he had thrown into the ocean as well.

He went in, and handed the keys to the man at the front desk, who was very impressed with how early he had returned the van.

"Did she treat you well?"

"Yes, she did. Thank you, for asking."

"Well, I'm glad, sir. Please come again soon."

"If ever I need a van again, I will."

Richard walked out of the dealership into the rain, which had lightened up a fair bit. He opened his umbrella and began the long walk back to his house. He had done it. He was nearly done, with the perfect crime. He just needed a few more finishing touches.

By the time he got back to the penthouse, it was after dark. Yvonne and Nathalie were puzzled by this.

"Where have you been all day, son?"

"Publisher. He took so long to actually show that we did not even get to the important things. We've decided to use Skype for the rest of our discussion."

"Good. That is the way it is supposed to be."

"Yeah. Is there any food left for me? I'm starving."

Nathalie took a plate of warm food from the microwave and gave it to her beloved father.

Richard sat at the kitchen counter eating his meal. The two women sat in the living room, watching a comedy programme.

Richard was pleased that everything was pretty much back to normal. He continued to eat, and as he did so, more and more memories of Sylvia came to mind.

He remembered them playing together, doing school work together, laughing together. Those were some of the fondest memories of his life, because in those moments that he spent with her, he remembered the feeling of a fever that burnt within his heart. A feeling that made it feel that everything was perfect in the world.

He then thought more to the night that they recently had sex together. That night was one that he knew he would never forget. To him, being inside her was a better experience than with any other woman.

Remembering how it felt to hold her breasts and watch them wobble about, he smiled and began to giggle softly to himself. To him, Sylvia was the ultimate woman back then.

However, his memory session came to an abrupt end, as he thought back to the day that he first professed his love for her and got rejected. His heart felt like it was being stabbed by a thousand blades, and reminded him of the pain she had caused him.

His final memory that night, was the memory of him, as he pulled the trigger on her. He was jolted back to reality, by that memory, because in all of his wildest dreams, he had never seen himself as a killer.

Richard had not finished his food, but he had now lost his appetite. He went and joined the two most important women in his life on the couch and the family sat around enjoying themselves, watching their favourite programmes.

Many hours past, and soon midnight struck. Nathalie went to sleep, and Yvonne soon followed suit of her, leaving Richard alone, to think to himself. He needed to forget all about Sylvia.

He needed to leave her in the past, where she belonged. That was who he was. A man who leaves his past behind him. But to do that, he needed to do a few more things.

He went to his office and poured himself a glass of brandy, then sat at his MacBook. He drafted out an email, to his publisher, telling her that the book was nearly done, and he would need it to be edited and have the cover art drawn up. Once the email was done, he went back to the book itself and began to finish off the last chapter.

He sat for so long, that eventually the sun rose behind him. The rainy weather was now at and end, and the sun shone brightly for the first time in many days. Richard looked out the window and thought to himself. *'Sylvia's smile was always brighter than the sun itself.'*

He was only about one page away from done, but he needed to do something else first. He needed to erase the footage of the van rental shop that he had visited the day before. He already had the frequency, all he needed was to scan for it and then erase it.

As easily as he had done in his building and the hotel, he got into the surveillance system of the rental shop and erased all the footage of the previous day. Things seemed too easy. He wondered to himself how other criminals got caught for this if he was getting away with it so easily.

He went straight back to the last chapter of the book and finished it off. He was pretty wiped out by this time, and he decided to go to sleep. He flopped onto his bed and was reawaken a minute later when the alarm went off. Nathalie came to his room and saw him lying there. She chose to leave him in peace and went to the kitchen to make something for herself.

Richard slept until around six at night, since he was exhausted and had not slept properly in days. When he woke up, he went to the kitchen and ate. Things had not been normal the past few days, but he was determined to make sure that everything went back to normal soon.

At ten, he went back to sleep, thinking to himself about going back to his normal life. He lay on his bed trying to fall asleep again, when his phone went off.

"Hello?"

"Hello. It's Mr Johnson."

Richard rose from his bed, surprised by his call. "Oh, yes. How are you?"

"Well, I'm still going through the loss of one of my best detectives so… I'm kind of peachy."

"Yeah. We all are."

"Yeah. But regardless, I thought you might like to know that Dylan Anderson has been arrested and charged with her murder, and for your shooting."

Richard smiled from his end of the line. He was relieved. It seemed like his plan had worked. Dylan was now going to be taking the fall for his handiwork.

"Oh. Okay. That's good. I suppose."

"Yes, it is indeed, Mr King."

"Okay, well, my novel is complete. It should be launched quite soon."

"Okay, that's good. I will definitely be picking one or two up, then."

Richard giggled and the two men had no more to say to one another that night, and so simply said 'good night'.

Richard was glad that his plan had worked out and now, he did not have to worry about being caught. He fell asleep and woke up a bit earlier than usual. He woke up in a very good mood and decided to make a culinary feast for his mother and Nathalie.

The two of them awoke to a succulent smell in the air. The smell of Richard's cooking. He had prepared a meal that was beyond that which he made on Christmas. Yvonne and Nathalie were very pleased to see Richard back to his cheerful self, and the family enjoyed their breakfast, together.

Richard later found himself at his MacBook again, but this time on Skype with his publisher. They discussed the book and they determined an approximate date for its launch. Richard then emailed her the book for editing and left all of it in her hands.

Nearly a month passed and the book was finally done. Editing, cover art, the works and the day came of the book launch. It was bigger than any of his other book launches before.

The turnout was massive and Richard eventually had to read a few pages of the first chapter to his audience. It all seemed to be going well, until the flood of memories came again. He took a very long pause as he tried to let them pass.

The memory of his pulling the trigger came last, just like all the times before. Richard was shocked. The memory had not come in the last month, and it was coming again, at the worst possible time.

Richard's pause was too long, and the audience grew curious as to what was going through his mind. As they wondered, Richard had another memory, one that he had not had since the day it happened. It was the memory of him burning Sylvia's corpse.

Richard, still on stage, began to cry and had a nervous breakdown. He fainted from the karma and fell to the ground. The crowd all gasped in shock and surrounded Richard, in concern. He was rushed to hospital, where he woke up a few hours later.

He tried to open his eyes, which seemed to just keep shutting by themselves. He caught a glimpse of Nathalie at his bedside and tried to use his arms, to get up.

"Arrgghh. Wha... What happened?"

"You passed out at the launch."

"Wha? Oh, no!"

"Stay down, Daddy."

Yvonne came into the room, and explained what happened to him. Richard did not understand. Everything had been going so well, why did it suddenly fall apart?

"We believe that it was a delayed reaction to the shooting. Since you never went through shock like this before."

"Yeah. I guess so then."

"But there was a great upside to your passing out earlier."

"Really, Mother, and what was that?"

Yvonne took out her tablet and held it up to Richard. He saw what seemed to be sales figures. It told him that in the five hours that he had been knocked out, they had sold every pre-launch copy of his book.

And hundreds of thousands of people had pre-ordered the book, in the United States alone.

It seemed like this book had achieved 'best seller' status already, and it was not even available in book stores yet.

Richard was discharged from the hospital about an hour later, since nothing was wrong with him. When the three of them reached the exit, they were ambushed by the press, the media and armies of sexually attractive women.

It took nearly two hours to walk to the car, which was just fifty metres away, but they finally got there and headed home. Richard was glad that the book was already doing so well, and with that, he could leave her behind, as a distant memory of the past, and tend to his future.

A few days passed and the book was going better than all his other books combined. Richard was receiving calls to be on programmes all over the world. He was now one of the most popular men alive, and a target for every woman alive.

He spent the next month or so travelling the world, with Yvonne and Nathalie, to be featured in all kinds of different programmes. His fame and fortune had increased nearly one hundred-fold; it was an incredible experience. Richard met and slept with so many women. Yvonne was approached by many, many men as well. Nathalie also enjoyed the time of her life. All three of them did.

The family finally returned to their home, in New York, and their lives seemed to go back to normal. Well, as normal as it was going to go back to being. They were now the most popular family in the world. There is no 'normal' when that happens.

Nathalie went back to school, Yvonne... well... Yvonne started looking for suitors for her son, and Richard went back to the place he loved. His bank, to focus on his real love. Money.

Getting back to his office was the most relieving experience he had had in months. His desk, his computer, his chair, it was all so perfect, it was like paradise.

After a couple of hours, however, Richard noticed something. This was the same place where he and Sylvia had been reunited. The thought shook him for a while, and kept him from doing any work.

The next day came, and it was a similar story. And the day after that, and the day after that, and the day after that. But with each day that passed, the thought lost more and more significance, until came a day where he thought about it and it just... did not matter the slightest bit.

The King family enjoyed their lives from there. Yvonne spent almost all of her time trying to find suitors for Richard to marry. From the biggest celebrities to the humblest of workers. One night, she was watching a programme called *Real Husbands of Hollywood*, and she said to Richard.

"What about this lady, my son?"

He looked at the screen to see the woman with her name and title beneath her. Jennifer White.

By now, he was used to these shenanigans and knew the best way to get his mother to stop was to just keep his mouth shut. He had to admit to himself, he did kind of like her, but no woman could take Sylvia's place in his heart. Even though he was the one who took her away from himself.

Life continued for the family. Yvonne eventually met a wonderful man by the name of Harold Black and the two of them had plans of getting married. Nathalie continued to pass at school, and was being chased by virtually every boy in the school, and Richard continued to work at his bank and got chased by practically every woman in the state.

Then, nearly a year after Sylvia's death, the time came for Dylan's trial. The family, of course, attended. The trial lasted nearly a week, but at the end, a jury found Dylan Anderson guilty of murder, shooting of Richard King, wrongful use of state resources and lying to officials.

However, due to the lack of evidence, besides his gun, he was only sentenced to seven years in prison.

Richard sat in the court and upon hearing the guilty verdict, he did not know how to feel. It meant that he had now gotten away with Sylvia's murder, but yet, it meant that he had just thrown an innocent man in prison. It was hard not to feel guilty about that, because he had taken far much more away from Dylan. His job, for instance. He would not be able to work for the Federal Bureau of Investigation ever again, for instance.

After court, Richard was asked to answer a few questions for a news crew.

"Mr King. How does it feel to see justice dealt to the man who shot you?"

"It feels good, but even with him behind bars, it does not right the wrong he did to me."

"Him shooting you?"

"No. He took away the woman that I loved. Sylvia Beckette."

"You two were in love?"

"Yes. Which is what I believed upset him, and drove him to commit this crime."

"Jealousy, you mean?"

"Yes. She was my inspiration for my last book. She was the woman I loved. All we wanted was to be happy. But now, there is nothing that can bring her back to me. As such, today was only a slight victory for me."

Richard began to shed tears, as he thought about Sylvia, and the news crew stopped asking him questions. Richard's tactic worked well for him. He fed the news people just enough truth, so that they would be able to swallow his biggest lie.

By playing the victim, and by planting evidence, Richard had gotten away with murder. He once said to Sylvia that he would write the perfect crime, but he had done far better. He had committed the perfect crime, and gotten away with it.

Richard and his family went back to their not-so-normal life, and just continued living. Yvonne and Nathalie never found out what Richard had done, and always believed that Dylan was a bad man, who had nearly killed Richard and succeeded at killing Sylvia.

Days went by, and the days turned into weeks and the weeks

turned into months. Richard occasionally was struck by thoughts and memories of the woman he had loved and murdered. He had days where he missed her and wanted her by his side, and he had to live with the fact the he had robbed himself and all other men of that experience.

He returned home one day, after dealing with a very difficult client at the bank, and had a beer. As he drank it, in his office, he finally came to terms with what he had done. He had killed Sylvia Beckette.

Incinerated her corpse. And framed someone for his actions.

If he were a career criminal, it would be something to be proud of. But as a legitimate accountant and an aspiring novelist… it was nothing to look back at, as a trophy. However, he knew that he could not change the past. He could only learn from it. This was what he had done and he would have to live with it for the rest of his life. There was nothing that he could say or do, even as the billionaire that he was, that could change the past or bring back the woman he wanted.

Like they say, there are somethings that money cannot by you, and this was one of those things.

Richard could never entirely forget her, no matter how many women he met. No matter how many women he slept with. No matter how big their breasts. No matter how smart their brains. No woman could ever take Sylvia's place in his heart, because he had lost it.

He lost his capability to love in that sense. And he could not be more pleased, because it meant that he would never go through the same insanity again. He was free of the torture of his heart and he would never need to go through the pain she had put him through again.

Because for the rest of his life…

He was free.

You see, Richard was like any other man. He was lured in by the promise of happiness that his heart gave him, and in the end, what his heart did, it turned our hero into a killer. A liar. A criminal.

All he did was love Sylvia, and she chose to break his heart, only to fall for him eight years later, which in the end, was the death of her.

The two of them were destined for each other, but the deception of the heart is what turned their story into a tragic tale of death.

If either of them had been smarter, and chose to obey their brains instead of their hearts, how do you think the tale of our heroes would have ended? Yet we, the human species, are always tempted to listen to our hearts. They always whisper in our ears a great promise of the ultimate happiness, in exchange for our blind obedience. In some cases, it makes good on that promise and in other cases not, but one thing it always does is, it brings some kind of pain and suffering.

It can be minor, such as if you discover that your partner cheated on you twenty years ago, to the major, such as if the one you love chooses someone else over you. It always brings some kind of pain, but not always gives you the happiness it promised.

Love... it is the stupidest and most futile of all human emotions. It prompts us to do the strangest and stupidest things, like throw one's self into prison for the freedom of the one you love, or get yourself killed just to spare the life of the one you love.

Love... in this day and age, tends to create monsters out of people. It can turn even the kindest man into a rapist or a killer. It can turn even the gentlest of women into arsonists and vandals.

And that is why we call love 'the greatest crime'.